PLAYING BY THE
GREEK'S RULES

PLAYING BY THE GREEK'S RULES

BY

SARAH MORGAN

First published in Great Britain 2015
by Mills & Boon, an imprint of Harlequin (UK) Limited,
Large Print edition 2015
Eton House, 18-24 Paradise Road,
Richmond, Surrey, TW9 1SR

© 2015 Sarah Morgan

ISBN: 978-0-263-25639-0

Harlequin (UK) Limited's policy is to use papers that
are natural, renewable and recyclable products and made
from wood grown in sustainable forests. The logging
and manufacturing processes conform to the legal
environmental regulations of the country of origin.

Printed and bound in Great Britain
by CPI Antony Rowe, Chippenham, Wiltshire

To the wonderful Joanne Grant,
for her enthusiasm, encouragement
and for always keeping the door open.

CHAPTER ONE

LILY PULLED HER hat down to shade her eyes from the burn of the hot Greek sun and took a large gulp from her water bottle. 'Never again.' She sat down on the parched, sunbaked earth and watched as her friend carefully brushed away dirt and soil from a small, carefully marked section of the trench. 'If I ever, *ever* mention the word "love" to you, I want you to bury me somewhere in this archaeological site and never dig me up again.'

'There is an underground burial chamber. I could dump you in there if you like.'

'Great idea. Stick a sign in the ground. *"Here lies Lily, who wasted years of her life studying the origin, evolution and behaviour of humans and still couldn't understand men".'* She gazed across the ruins of the ancient city of Aptera to the sea beyond. They were high on a plateau. Behind them, the jagged beauty of the White Mountains shimmered in the heat and in front lay the sparkling blue of the Sea of Crete. The beauty of it usually lifted her mood, but not today.

Brittany sat up and wiped her brow with her forearm. 'Stop beating yourself up. The guy is a lying, cheating rat bastard.' Reaching for her backpack, she glanced across the site to the group of men who were deep in conversation. 'Fortunately for all of us he's flying back to London tomorrow to his wife. And all I can say to that is, God help the woman.'

Lily covered her face with her hands. 'Don't say the word "wife". I am a terrible person.'

'Hey!' Brittany's voice was sharp. 'He told you he was single. He *lied*. The responsibility is all his. After tomorrow you won't have to see him again and I won't have to struggle not to kill him.'

'What if she finds out and ends their marriage?'

'Then she might have the chance of a decent life with someone who respects her. Forget him, Lily.'

How could she forget when she couldn't stop going over and over it in her head?

Had there been signs she'd missed?

Had she asked the wrong questions?

Was she so desperate to find someone special that she'd ignored obvious signs?

'I was planning our future. We were going to spend August touring the Greek Islands. That was before he pulled out a family photo from his wallet instead of his credit card. Three little kids wrapped around their dad like bindweed. He should have been taking them on holiday, not me! I can't bear it. How could I have made such an appalling error of judgement? That is a line I *never* cross. Family is sacrosanct to me. If you asked me to pick between family and money, I'd pick family every time.' It crossed her mind that right now she had neither. No money. No family. 'I don't know which is worse—the fact that he clearly didn't know me *at all*, or the fact that when I checked him against my list he was perfect.'

'You have a list?'

Lily felt herself grow pink. 'It's my attempt to be objective. I have a really strong desire for permanent roots. Family.' She thought about the emotional wasteland of her past and felt a sense of failure. Was the future going to look the same way? 'When you want something badly it can distort your decision-making process, so I've put in some layers of protection for myself. I know the basic qualities I need in a man to be happy. I never date anyone who doesn't score highly on my three points.'

Brittany looked intrigued. 'Big wallet, big shoulders and big—'

'No! And you are appalling.' Despite her misery, Lily laughed. 'First, he has to be affectionate. I'm not interested in a man who can't show his feelings. Second, he has to be honest, but short of getting him to take a lie detector test I don't know how to check that one. I thought Professor Ashurst was honest. I'm never calling him David again, by the way.' She allowed herself one glance at the visiting archaeologist who had dazzled her during their short, ill-fated relationship. 'You're right. He's a rat pig.'

'I didn't call him a rat pig. I called him a rat b—'

'I know what you called him. I never use that word.'

'You should. It's surprisingly therapeutic. But we shouldn't be wasting this much time talking about him. Professor Asshat is history, like this stuff we're digging up.'

'I can't believe you called him that.'

'You should be calling him far worse. What's the third thing on your list?'

'I want a man with strong family values. He has to want a family. But not several different families at the same time. Now I know why he gave off all those signals about being a family man. Because he already *was* a family man.' Lily descended into gloom. 'My checklist is seriously flawed.'

'Not necessarily. You need a more reliable test for honesty and you should maybe add "single" to your list, that's all. You need to chill. Stop looking for a relationship and have some fun. Keep it casual.'

'You're talking about sex? That doesn't work for me.' Lily took another sip of water. 'I have to be in love with a guy to sleep with him. The two are welded together for me. How about you?'

'No. Sex is sex. Love is love. One is fun and the other is to be avoided at all costs.'

'I don't think like that. There is something wrong with me.'

'There's nothing wrong with you. It's not a crime to want a relationship. It just means you get your heart broken more than the average person.' Brittany pushed her hat back from her face. 'I can't believe how hot it is. It's not even ten o'clock and already I'm boiling like a lobster.'

'And you know all about lobsters, coming from Maine. It's summer and this is Crete. What did you expect?'

'Right now I'd give anything for a few hours back home. I'm not used to summers that fry your skin from your body. I keep wanting to remove another layer of clothing.'

'You've spent summers at digs all over the Mediterranean.'

'And I moaned at each and every one.' Brittany stretched out her legs and Lily felt a flash of envy.

'You look like Lara Croft in those shorts. You have amazing legs.'

'Too much time hiking in inhospitable lands searching for ancient relics. I want your gorgeous blonde hair.' Brittany's hair, the colour of polished oak, was gathered up from her neck in a ponytail. Despite the hat, her neck was already showing signs of the sun. 'Listen, don't waste another thought or tear on that man. Come out with us tonight. We're going to the official opening of the new wing at the archaeological museum and afterwards we're going to try out that new bar on the waterfront. My spies tell me that Professor Asshat won't be there, so it's going to be a great evening.'

'I can't. The agency rang this morning and offered me an emergency cleaning job.'

'Lily, you have a masters in archaeology. You shouldn't be taking these random jobs.'

'My research grant doesn't pay off my college loans and I want to be debt free. And anyway, I love cleaning. It relaxes me.'

'You love cleaning? You're like a creature from another planet.'

'There's nothing more rewarding than turning someone's messy house into a shiny home, but I do wish the job wasn't tonight. The opening would have been fun. A great excuse to wash the mud off my knees and dress up, not to mention seeing all those artefacts in one place. Never mind. I'll focus on the money. They're paying me an emergency rate for tonight.'

'Cleaning is an emergency?'

Lily thought about the state of some of the houses she cleaned. 'Sometimes, but in this case it's more that the owner decided to arrive without notice. He spends most of his time in the US.' She dug in her bag for more sunscreen. 'Can you imagine being so rich you can't quite decide which of your many properties you are going to sleep in?'

'What's his name?'

'No idea. The company is very secretive. We have to arrive at a certain time and then his security team will let us in. Four hours later I add a gratifyingly large sum of money to my bank account and that's the end of it.'

'Four hours? It's going to take five of you four hours to clean one house?' Brittany paused with the water halfway to her mouth. 'What is this place? A Minoan palace?'

'A villa. It's big. She said I'd be given a floor

plan when I arrive, which I have to return when I leave and I'm not allowed to make copies.'

'A *floor plan*?' Brittany choked on her water. 'Now I'm intrigued. Can I come with you?'

'Sure—' Lily threw her a look '—because scrubbing out someone's shower is so much more exciting than having cocktails on the terrace of the archaeological museum while the sun sets over the Aegean.'

'It's the Sea of Crete.'

'Technically it's still the Aegean, and either way I'm missing a great party to scrub a floor. I feel like Cinderella. So what about you? Are you going to meet someone tonight and do something about your dormant love life?'

'I don't have a love life, I have a sex life, which is not at all dormant fortunately.'

Lily felt a twinge of envy. 'Maybe you're right. I need to lighten up and use men for sex instead of treating every relationship as if it's going to end in confetti. You were an only child, weren't you? Did you ever wish you had brothers or sisters?'

'No, but I grew up on a small island. The whole place felt like a massive extended family. Everyone knew everything, from the age you first walked, to whether you had all A's on your report card.'

'Sounds blissful.' Lily heard the wistful note in her own voice. 'Because I was such a sickly kid and hard work to look after, no one took me for long. My eczema was terrible when I was little and I was always covered in creams and bandages and other yucky stuff. I wasn't exactly your poster baby. No one wanted a kid who got sick. I was about as welcome as a stray puppy with fleas.'

'Crap, Lily, you're making me tear up and I'm not even a sentimental person.'

'Forget it. Tell me about your family instead.' She loved hearing about other people's families, about the complications, the love, the experiences woven into a shared history. To her, family seemed like a multicoloured sweater, with all the different coloured strands of wool knitted into something whole and wonderful that gave warmth and protection from the cold winds of life.

She picked absently at a thread hanging from the hem of her shorts. It felt symbolic of her life. She was a single fibre, loose, bound to nothing.

Brittany took another mouthful of water and adjusted the angle of her hat. 'We're a normal American family, I guess. Whatever that is. My parents were divorced when I was ten. My mom hated living on an island. Eventually she remarried and moved to Florida. My dad was an engineer and he spent all his time working on oil rigs around the world. I lived with my grandmother on Puffin Island.'

'Even the name is adorable.' Lily tried to imagine growing up on a place called Puffin Island. 'Were you close to your grandmother?'

'Very. She died a few years ago, but she left me her cottage on the beach so I'd always have a home. I take several calls a week from people wanting to buy the place but I'm never going to sell.' Brittany poked her trowel into the ground. 'My grandmother called it Castaway Cottage. When I was little I asked her if a castaway ever lived there and she said it was for people lost in life, not at sea. She believed it had healing properties.'

Lily didn't laugh. 'I might need to spend a month there. I need to heal.'

'You'd be welcome. A friend of mine is staying at the moment. We use it as a refuge. It's the best place on earth and I always feel close to my grandmother when I'm there. You can use it any time, Lil.'

'Maybe I will. I still need to decide what I'm going to do in August.'

'You know what you need? Rebound sex. Sex

for the fun of it, without all the emotional crap that goes with relationships.'

'I've never had rebound sex. I'd fall in love.'

'So pick someone you couldn't possibly fall in love with in a million years. Someone with exceptional bedroom skills, but nothing else to commend him. Then you can't possibly be at risk.' She broke off as Spyros, one of the Greek archaeologists from the local university, strolled across to them. 'Go away, Spy, this is girl talk.'

'Why do you think I'm joining you? It's got to be more interesting than the conversation I just left.' He handed Lily a can of chilled Diet Coke. 'He's a waste of space, *theé mou*.' His voice was gentle and she coloured, touched by his kindness.

'I know, I know.' She lifted the weight of her hair from her neck, wishing she'd worn it up. 'I'll get over it.'

Spy dropped to his haunches next to her. 'Want me to help you get over him? I heard something about rebound sex. I'm here for you.'

'No thanks. You're a terrible flirt. I don't trust you.'

'Hey, this is about sex. You don't need to trust me.' He winked at her. 'What you need is a real man. A Greek man who knows how to make you feel like a woman.'

'Yeah, yeah, I know the joke. You're going to hand me your laundry and tell me to wash it. This is why you're not going to be my rebound guy. I am not washing your socks.' But Lily was laughing as she snapped the top of the can. Maybe she didn't have a family, but she had good friends. 'You're forgetting that when I'm not cleaning the villas of the rich or hanging out here contributing nothing to my college fund, I work for the ultimate in Greek manhood.'

'Ah yes.' Spyros smiled. 'Nik Zervakis. Head of the mighty ZervaCo. Man of men. Every woman's fantasy.'

'Not mine. He doesn't tick a single box on my list.'

Spy raised his eyebrows and Brittany shook her head. 'You don't want to know. Go on, Lily, dish the dirt on Zervakis. I want to know everything from his bank balance to how he got that incredible six pack I saw in those sneaky photos of him taken in that actress's swimming pool.'

'I don't know much about him, except that he's super brilliant and expects everyone around him to be super brilliant, too, which makes him pretty intimidating. Fortunately he spends most of his time in San Francisco or New York so he isn't around much. I've been doing this internship for two months and in that time two personal assistants have left. It's a good job he has a big human resources department because I can tell you he gets through *a lot* of human resources in the average working week. And don't even start me on the girlfriends. I need a spreadsheet to keep it straight in my head.'

'What happened to the personal assistants?'

'Both of them resigned because of the pressure. The workload is inhuman and he isn't easy to work for. He has this way of looking at you that makes you wish you could teleport. But he *is* very attractive. He isn't my type so I didn't pay much attention, but the women talk about him all the time.'

'I still don't understand why you're working there.'

'I'm trying different things. My research grant ends this month and I don't know if I want to carry on doing this. I'm exploring other options. Museum work doesn't pay much and anyway, I don't want to live in a big city. I could never teach—' She shrugged, depressed by the options. 'I don't know what to do.'

'You're an expert in ceramics and you've made some beautiful pots.'

'That's a hobby.'

'You're creative and artistic. You should do something with that.'

'It isn't practical to think I can make a living that way and dreaming doesn't pay the bills.' She finished her drink. 'Sometimes I wish I'd read law, not archaeology, except that I don't think I'm cut out for office work. I'm not good with technology. I broke the photocopier last week and the coffee machine hates me, but apparently having ZervaCo on your résumé makes prospective employers sit up. It shows you have staying power. If you can work there and not be intimidated, you're obviously robust. And before you tell me that an educated woman shouldn't allow herself to be intimidated by a guy, try meeting him.'

Spyros rose to his feet. 'Plenty of people would be intimidated by Nik Zervakis. There are some who say his name along with the gods.'

Brittany pushed her water bottle back into her backpack. 'Those would be the people whose salary he pays, or the women he sleeps with.'

Lily took off her hat and fanned herself. 'His security team is briefed to keep them away from him. We are not allowed to put any calls through to him unless the name is on an approved list and that list changes pretty much every week. I have terrible trouble keeping up.'

'So his protection squad is there to protect him from women?' Brittany looked fascinated. 'Unreal.'

'I admire him. They say his emotions have never played a part in anything he does, business or pleasure. He is the opposite of everything I am. No one has ever dumped him or made him feel less of a person and he always knows what to say in any situation.' She glanced once across the heat-baked ruins of the archaeological site towards the man who had lied so glibly. Thinking of all the things she could have said and hadn't plunged her into another fit of gloom. 'I'm going to try and be more like Nik Zervakis.'

Brittany laughed. 'You're kidding, right?'

'No, I'm not kidding. He is like an ice machine. I want to be like that. How about you? Have either of you ever been in love?'

'No!' Spy looked alarmed, but Brittany didn't answer. Instead she stared sightlessly across the plateau to the ocean.

'Brittany?' Lily prompted her. 'Have you been in love?'

'Not sure.' Her friend's voice was husky. 'Maybe.'

'Wow. Ball-breaking Brittany, in love?' Spy raised his eyebrows. 'Did you literally fire an arrow through his heart?' He spread his hands as Lily glared at him. 'What? She's a Bronze Age weapons expert and a terrifyingly good archer. It's a logical suggestion.'

Lily ignored him. 'What makes you think you might have been in love? What were the clues?'

'I married him.'

Spyros doubled up with soundless laughter and Lily stared.

'You—? Okay. Well that's a fairly big clue right there.'

'It was a mistake.' Brittany tugged the trowel out of the ground. 'When I make mistakes I make sure they're *big*. I guess you could call it a whirlwind romance.'

'That sounds more like a hurricane than a whirlwind. How long did it last?'

Brittany stood up and brushed dust off her legs. 'Ten days. Spy, if you don't wipe that smile off your face I'm going to kick you into this trench and cover your corpse with a thick layer of dirt and shards of pottery.'

'You mean ten *years*,' Lily said and Brittany shook her head.

'No. I mean days. We made it through the honeymoon without killing each other.'

Lily felt her mouth drop open and closed it again quickly. 'What happened?'

'I let my emotions get in the way of making sane decisions.' Brittany gave a faint smile. 'I haven't fallen in love since.'

'Because you learned how not to do it. You didn't go and make the same mistake again and again. Give me some tips.'

'I can't. Avoiding emotional entanglement came naturally after I met Zach.'

'Sexy name.'

'Sexy guy.' She shaded her eyes from the sun. 'Sexy rat bastard guy.'

'Another one,' Lily said gloomily. 'But you were young and everyone is allowed to make mistakes when they're young. Not only do I not have that excuse, but I'm a habitual offender. I should be locked up until I'm safe to be rehabilitated. I need to be taken back to the store and reprogrammed.'

'You do not need to be reprogrammed.' Brittany stuffed her trowel into the front of her backpack. 'You're warm, friendly and lovable. That's what guys like about you.'

'That and the fact it takes one glance to know you'd look great naked,' Spy said affably.

Lily turned her back on him. 'Warm, friendly and lovable are great qualities for a puppy, but not so great for a woman. They say a person can change, don't they? Well, I'm going to change.'

She scrambled to her feet. 'I am not falling in love again. I'm going to take your advice and have rebound sex.'

'Good plan.' Spy glanced at his watch. 'You get your clothes off, I'll get us a room.'

'Not funny.' Lily glared at him. 'I am going to pick someone I don't know, don't feel anything for and couldn't fall in love with in a million years.'

Brittany looked doubtful. 'Now I'm second-guessing myself. Coming from you it sounds like a recipe for disaster.'

'It's going to be perfect. All I have to do is find a man who doesn't tick a single box on my list and have sex with him. It can't possibly go wrong. I'm going to call it Operation Ice Maiden.'

Nik Zervakis stood with his back to the office, staring at the glittering blue of the sea while his assistant updated him. 'Did he call?'

'Yes, exactly as you predicted. How do you always know these things? I would have lost my nerve days ago with those sums of money involved. You don't even break out in a sweat.'

Nik could have told him the deal wasn't about money, it was about power. 'Did you call the lawyers?'

'They're meeting with the team from Lexos first thing tomorrow. So it's done. Congratulations, boss. The US media have turned the phones red-hot asking for interviews.'

'It's not over until the deal is signed. When that happens I'll put out a statement, but no interviews.' Nik felt some of the tension leave his shoulders. 'Did you make a reservation at The Athena?'

'Yes, but you have the official opening of the new museum wing first.'

Nik swore softly and swung round. 'I'd forgotten. Do you have a briefing document on that?'

His PA paled. 'No, boss. All I know is that the wing has been specially designed to display Minoan antiquities in one place. You were invited to the final meeting of the project team but you were in San Francisco.'

'Am I supposed to give a speech?'

'They're hoping you will agree to say a few words.'

'I can manage a few words, but they'll be unrelated to Minoan antiquities.' Nik loosened his tie. 'Run me through the schedule.'

'Vassilis will have the car here at six-fifteen, which should allow you time to go back to the villa and change. You're picking up Christina on the way and your table is booked for nine p.m.'

'Why not pick her up after I've changed?'

'That would have taken time you don't have.'

Nik couldn't argue with that. The demands of his schedule had seen off three assistants in the last six months. 'There was something else?'

The man shifted uncomfortably. 'Your father called. Several times. He said you weren't picking up your phone and asked me to relay a message.'

Nik flicked open the button at the neck of his shirt. 'Which was?'

'He wants to remind you that his wedding is next weekend. He thinks you've forgotten.'

Nik stilled. *He hadn't forgotten.* 'Anything else?'

'He is looking forward to having you at the celebrations. He wanted me to remind you that of all the riches in this world, family is the most valuable.'

Nik, whose sentiments on that topic were a matter of public record, made no comment.

He wondered why anyone would see a fourth wedding as a cause for celebration. To him, it shrieked of someone who hadn't learned his lesson the first three times. 'I will call him from the car.'

'There was one more thing—' The man backed towards the door like someone who knew he was going to need to make a rapid exit. 'He said to make sure you knew that if you don't come, you'll break his heart.'

It was a statement typical of his father. Emotional. Unguarded.

Reflecting that it was that very degree of sentimentality that had made his father the victim of three costly divorces, Niklaus strolled to his desk. 'Consider the message delivered.'

As the door closed he turned back to the window, staring over the midday sparkle of the sea.

Exasperation mingled with frustration and beneath that surface response lay darker, murkier emotions he had no wish to examine. He wasn't given to introspection and he believed that the past was only useful when it informed the future, so finding himself staring down into a swirling mass of long-ignored memories was an unwelcome experience.

Despite the air conditioning, sweat beaded on his forehead and he strode across his office and pulled a bottle of iced water from the fridge.

Why should it bother him that his father was marrying again?

He was no longer an idealistic nine-year-old, shattered by a mother's betrayal and driven by a deep longing for order and security.

He'd learned to make his own security. Emotionally he was an impenetrable fortress. He would never allow a relationship to explode the world from under his feet. He didn't believe in love and he saw marriage as expensive and pointless.

Unfortunately his father, an otherwise intelligent man, didn't share his views. He'd managed to build a successful business from nothing but the fruits of the land around him, but for some reason he had failed to apply that same intellect to his love life.

Nik reflected that if he approached business the way his father approached relationships, he would be broke.

As far as he could see his father performed no risk analysis, gave no consideration to the financial implications of each of his romantic whims and approached each relationship with the romantic optimism entirely inappropriate for a man on his fourth marriage.

Nik's attempts to encourage at least some degree of circumspection had been dismissed as cynical.

To make the situation all the more galling, the last time they'd met for dinner his father had actually lectured him on his lifestyle as if Nik's lack of divorces suggested a deep character flaw.

Nik closed his eyes briefly and wondered how everything in his business life could run so smoothly while his family was as messy as a dropped pan of spaghetti. The truth was he'd rather endure the twelve labours of Hercules than attend another of his father's weddings.

This time he hadn't met his father's intended bride and he didn't want to. He failed to see what he would bring to the proceedings other than grim disapproval and he didn't want to spoil the day.

Weddings depressed him. All the champagne bubbles in the world couldn't conceal the fact that two people were paying a fortune for the privilege of making a very public mistake.

Lily dumped her bag in the marble hallway and tried to stop her jaw from dropping.

Palatial didn't begin to describe it. Situated on the headland overlooking the sparkling blue of the sea, Villa Harmonia epitomised calm, high-end luxury.

Wondering where the rest of the team were, she wandered out onto the terrace.

Tiny paths wound down through the tumbling gardens to a private cove with a jetty where a platform gave direct swimming access to the sea.

'I've died and gone to heaven.' Disturbed from

her trance by the insistent buzz of her phone, she dug it out of her pocket. Her simple uniform was uncomfortably tight, courtesy of all the delicious thyme honey and Greek yoghurt she'd consumed since arriving in Crete. Her phone call turned out to be the owner of the cleaning company, who told her that the rest of the team had been involved in an accident and wouldn't make it.

'Oh no, are they hurt?' On hearing that no one was in hospital but that the car was totalled, Lily realised she was going to be on her own with this job. 'So if it normally takes four of us four hours, how is one person going to manage?'

'Concentrate on the living areas and the master suite. Pay particular attention to the bathroom.'

Resigned to doing the best she could by herself, Lily set to work. Choosing Mozart from her soundtrack, she pushed in her earbuds and sang her way through *The Magic Flute* while she brushed and mopped the spacious living area.

Whoever lived here clearly didn't have children, she thought as she plumped cushions on deep white sofas and polished glass tables. Everything was sophisticated and understated.

Realising that dreaming would get her fired, Lily hummed her way up the curving staircase to the master bedroom and stopped dead.

The tiny, airless apartment she shared with Brittany had a single bed so narrow she'd twice fallen out of it in her sleep. *This* bed, by contrast, was large enough to sleep a family of six comfortably. It was positioned to take advantage of the incredible view across the bay and Lily stood, drooling with envy, imagining how it must feel to sleep in a bed this size. How many times could you roll over before finding yourself on the floor? If it were hers, she'd spread out like a starfish.

Glancing quickly over her shoulder to check there was no sign of the security team, she unclipped her phone from her pocket and took a photo of the bed and the view.

One day, she texted Brittany, I'm going to have sex in a bed like this.

Brittany texted back, I don't care about the bed, just give me the man who owns it.

With a last wistful look at the room, Lily tucked her phone carefully into her bag and strolled into the bathroom. A large tub was positioned next to a wall of glass, offering the owner an uninterrupted view of the ocean. The only way to clean something so large was to climb inside it, so she did that, extra careful not to slip.

When it was gleaming, she turned her attention to the large walk-in shower. There was a sophisticated control panel on the wall and she looked at it doubtfully. Remembering her disastrous experience with the photocopier and the coffee machine, she was reluctant to touch anything, but what choice was there?

Lifting her hand, she pressed a button cautiously and gasped as a powerful jet of freezing water hit her from the opposite wall.

Breathless, she slammed her hand on another button to try and stop the flow but that turned on a different jet and she was blasted with water until her hair and clothes were plastered to her body and she couldn't see. She thumped the wall blindly and was alternately scalded and frozen until finally she managed to turn off the jets. Panting, her hair and clothes plastered to her body, she sank to the floor while she tried to get her breath back, shivering and dripping like a puppy caught in the rain.

'I hate, hate, *hate* technology.' She pushed her hair back from her face, took it in her hands and twisted it into a rope, squeezing to remove as much of the water as she could. Then she stood up, but her uniform was dripping and stuck to her skin. If she walked back through the villa like this, she'd drip water everywhere and she didn't have time to clean the place again.

Peeling off her uniform, she was standing in her underwear wringing out the water when she heard a sound from the bedroom.

Assuming it must be one of the security team, she gave a whimper of horror. 'Hello? If there's anyone out there, don't come in for a moment because I'm just—' She stilled as a woman appeared in the doorway.

She was perfectly groomed, her slender body sheathed in a silk dress the colour of coral, her mouth a sheen of blended lipstick and lip-gloss.

Lily had never felt more outclassed in her life.

'Nik?' The woman spoke over her shoulder, her tone icy. 'Your sex drive is, of course, a thing of legend but for the record it's always a good idea to remove the last girlfriend before installing a new one.'

'What are you talking about?' The male voice came from the bedroom, deep, bored and instantly recognisable.

Still shivering from the impact of the cold water, Lily closed her eyes and wondered if any of the buttons on the control panel operated an ejector seat.

Now she knew who owned the villa.

Moments later he appeared in the doorway and Lily peered through soaked lashes and had her second ever look at Nik Zervakis. Confronted by more good looks and sex appeal than she'd ever seen concentrated in one man before, her tummy tumbled and she felt as if she were plunging downhill on a roller coaster.

He stood, legs braced apart, his handsome face blank of expression as if finding a semi-naked woman in his shower wasn't an event worthy of an emotional response. 'Well?'

That was all he was going to say?

Braced for an explosion of volcanic proportions, Lily gulped. 'I can explain—'

'I wish you would.' The woman's voice turned from ice to acid and her expensively shod foot tapped rhythmically on the floor. 'This should be worth hearing.'

'I'm the cleaner—'

'Of course you are. Because "cleaners" always end up naked in the client's shower.' Vibrating with anger, she turned the beam of her angry glare onto the man next to her. 'Nik?'

'Yes?'

Her mouth tightened into a thin, dangerous line. 'Who is she?'

'You heard her. She's the cleaner.'

'*Obviously* she's lying.' The woman bristled.

'No doubt she's been here all day, sleeping off the night before.'

His only response to that was a faint narrowing of those spectacular dark eyes.

Recalling someone warning her on her first day with his company that Nik Zervakis was at his most dangerous when he was quiet, Lily felt her anxiety levels rocket but apparently her concerns weren't shared by his date for the evening, who continued to berate him.

'Do you know the worst thing about this? Not that you have a wandering eye, but that your eye wanders to someone as fat as her.'

'*Excuse* me? I'm not fat.' Lily tried vainly to cover herself with the soaking uniform. 'I'll have you know that my BMI is within normal range.'

But the woman wasn't listening. 'Was she the reason you were late picking me up? I *warned* you, Nik, no games, and yet you do this to me. Well, you gambled and you lost because I don't do second chances, especially this early in a relationship and if you can't be bothered to give an explanation then I can't be bothered to ask for one.' Without giving him the chance to respond, his date stalked out of the room and Lily flinched in time with each furious tap of those skyscraper heels.

She stood in awkward silence, her feelings bruised and her spirits drenched in cold water and guilt. 'She's very upset.'

'Yes.'

'Er—is she coming back?'

'I sincerely hope not.'

Lily wanted to say that he was well rid of her, but decided that protecting her job was more important than honesty. 'I'm *really* sorry—'

'Don't be. It wasn't your fault.'

Knowing that wasn't quite true, she squirmed. 'If I hadn't had an accident, I would have had my clothes on when she walked into the room.'

'An accident? I've never considered my shower to be a place of danger but apparently I was wrong about that.' He eyed the volume of water on the floor and her drenched clothing. 'What happened?'

'Your shower is like the flight deck of a jumbo jet, that's what happened!' Freezing and soaked, Lily couldn't stop her teeth chattering. 'There are no instructions.'

'I don't need instructions.' His gaze slid over her with slow, disturbing thoroughness. 'I'm familiar with the workings of my own shower.'

'Well I'm not! I had no idea which buttons to press.'

'So you thought you'd press all of them? If you ever find yourself on the flight deck of a Boeing 747 I suggest you sit on your hands.'

'It's not f-f-funny. I'm soaking wet and I didn't know you were going to come home early.'

'I apologise.' Irony gleamed in those dark eyes. 'I'm not in the habit of notifying people of my movements in advance. Have you finished cleaning or do you want me to show you which buttons to press?'

Lily summoned as much dignity as she could in the circumstances. 'Your shower is clean. Extra clean, because I wiped myself around it personally.' Anxious to make her exit as fast as possible, she kept her eyes fixed on the door and away from that tall, powerful frame. 'Are you sure she isn't coming back?'

'No.'

Lily paused, torn between relief and guilt. 'I've ruined another relationship.'

'Another?' Dark eyebrows lifted. 'It's a common occurrence?'

'You have no idea. Look—if it would help I could call my employer and ask her to vouch for me.' Her voice tailed off as she realised that would mean confessing she'd been caught half naked in the shower.

He gave a faint smile. 'Unless you have a very liberal-minded employer, you might want to re-think that idea.'

'There must be some way I can fix this. I've ruined your date, although for the record I don't think she's a very kind person so she might not be good for you in the long term and with a body that bony she won't be very cuddly for your children.' She caught his eye. 'Are you laughing at me?'

'No, but the ability to cuddle children isn't high on my list of necessary female attributes.' He flung his jacket carelessly over the back of a sofa that was bigger than her bed at home.

She stared in fascination, wondering if he cared at all that his date had walked out. 'As a matter of interest, why didn't you defend yourself?'

'Why would I defend myself?'

'You could have explained yourself and then she would have forgiven you.'

'I never explain myself. And anyway—' he shrugged '—you had already given her an explanation.'

'I don't think she saw me as a credible witness. It might have sounded better coming from you.'

He stood, legs spread, his powerful shoulders blocking the doorway. 'I assume you told her the truth? You're the cleaner?'

'Of course I told her the truth.'

'Then there was nothing I could have added to your story.'

In his position she would have died of humiliation, but he seemed supremely indifferent to the fact he'd been publicly dumped. 'You don't seem upset.'

'Why would I be upset?'

'Because most people are upset when a relationships ends.'

He smiled. 'I'm not one of those.'

Lily felt a flash of envy. 'You're not even a teeny tiny bit sad?'

'I'm not familiar with that unit of measurement but no, I'm not even a "teeny tiny" bit sad. To be sad I'd have to care and I don't care.'

To be sad I'd have to care and I don't care.

Brilliant, Lily thought. *Why* couldn't she have said that to Professor Ashurst when he'd given her that fake sympathy about having hurt her? She needed to memorise it for next time. 'Excuse me a moment.' Leaving a dripping trail behind her, she shot past him, scrabbled in her bag and pulled out a notebook.

'What are you doing?'

'I'm writing down what you said. Whenever I'm dumped I never know the right thing to say, but next time it happens I'm going to say *exactly* those words in exactly that tone instead of producing enough tears to power a water feature at Versailles.' She scribbled, dripping water onto her notebook and smearing the ink.

'Being "dumped" is something that happens to you often?'

'Often enough. I fall in love, I get my heart broken, it's a cycle I'm working on breaking.' She wished she hadn't said anything. Although she was fairly open with people, she drew the line at making public announcements about not being easy to love.

That was her secret.

'How many times have you fallen in love?'

'So far?' She shook the pen with frustration as the ink stalled on the damp page, 'Three times.'

'*Cristo*, that's unbelievable.'

'Thanks for not making me feel better. I bet you've never been unlucky in love, have you?'

'I've never been in love at all.'

Lily digested that. 'You've never met the right person.'

'I don't believe in love.'

'You—' She rocked back on her heels, her attention caught. 'So what do you believe in?'

'Money, influence and power.' He shrugged. 'Tangible, measurable goals.'

'You can measure power and influence? Don't tell me—you stamp your foot and it registers on the Richter scale.'

He loosened his tie. 'You'd be surprised.'

'I'm already surprised. Gosh, you are *so* cool. You are my new role model.' Finally she managed to coax ink from the pen. 'It is never too late to change. From now on I'm all about tangible, measurable goals, too. As a matter of interest, what is your goal in relationships?'

'Orgasm.' He gave a slow smile and she felt herself turn scarlet.

'Right. Well, that serves me right for asking a stupid question. That's definitely a measurable goal. You're obviously able to be cold and ruthlessly detached when it comes to relationships. I'm aiming for that. I've dripped all over your floor. Be careful not to slip.'

He was leaning against the wall, watching her with amusement. 'This is what you look like when you're being cold and ruthlessly detached?'

'I haven't actually started yet, but the moment my radar warns me I might be in danger of falling for the wrong type, *bam*—' she punched the air with her fist '—I'm going to turn on my freezing side. From now on I have armour around my heart. Kevlar.' She gave him a friendly smile. 'You think I'm crazy, right? All this is natural to you. But it isn't to me. This is the first stage of my personality transplant. I'd love to do the whole thing under anaesthetic and wake up all new and perfect, but that isn't possible so I'm trying to embrace the process.'

A vibrating noise caught her attention and she glanced across the room towards his jacket. When he didn't move, she looked at him expectantly. 'That's your phone.'

He was still watching her, his gaze disturbingly intent. 'Yes.'

'You're not going to answer it?' She scrambled to her feet, still clutching the towel. 'It might be her, asking for your forgiveness.'

'I'm sure it is, which is why I don't intend to answer it.'

Lily absorbed that with admiration. 'This is a perfect example of why I need to be like you and not like me. If that had been my phone, I would have answered it and when whoever was on the end apologised for treating me badly, I would have told him it was fine. I would have forgiven them.'

'You're right,' he said. 'You do need help. What's your name?'

She shifted, her wet feet sticking to the floor. 'Lily. Like the flower.'

'You look familiar. Have we met before?'

Lily felt the colour pour into her cheeks. 'I've been working as an intern at your company two days a week for the past couple of months. I'm second assistant to your personal assistant.' *I'm the one who broke the photocopier and the coffee machine.*

Dark eyebrows rose. 'We've met?'

'No. I've only seen you once in person. I don't count the time I was hiding in the bathroom.'

'You hid in the bathroom?'

'You were on a firing spree. I didn't want to be noticed.'

'So you work for me two days a week, and on the other three days you're working as a cleaner?'

'No, I only do that job in the evenings. The other three days I'm doing fieldwork up at Aptera for the summer. But that's almost finished. I've reached a crossroads in my life and I've no idea which direction to take.'

'Fieldwork?' That sparked his interest. 'You're an archaeologist?'

'Yes, I'm part of a project funded by the university but that part doesn't pay off my massive college loans so I have other jobs.'

'How much do you know about Minoan antiquities?'

Lily blinked. 'Probably more than is healthy for a woman of twenty-four.'

'Good. Get back into the bathroom and dry yourself off while I find you a dress. Tonight I have to open the new wing of the museum. You're coming with me.'

'Me? Don't you have a date?'

'I had a date,' he said smoothly. 'As you're partially responsible for the fact she's no longer here, you're coming in her place.'

'But—' She licked her lips. 'I'm supposed to be cleaning your villa.'

His gaze slid from her face to the wash of water covering the bathroom floor. 'I'd say you've done a pretty thorough job. By the time we get home, the flood will have spread down the stairs and across the living areas, so it will clean itself.'

Lily gave a gurgle of laughter. She wondered if any of his employees realised he had a sense of humour. 'You're not going to fire me?'

'You should have more confidence in yourself. If you have knowledge of Minoan artefacts then I still have a use for you and I never fire people who are useful.' He reached for the towel and tugged it off, leaving her clad only in her soaking wet underwear.

'What are you doing?' She gave a squeak of embarrassment and snatched at the towel but he held it out of reach.

'Stop wriggling. I can't be the first man to see you half naked.'

'Usually I'm in a relationship when a man sees me naked. And being stared at is very unnerving, especially when you've been called fat by someone who looks like a toast rack—' Lily broke off as he turned and strolled away from her. She didn't know whether to be relieved or affronted. 'If you want to know my size you could ask me!'

He reached for his phone and dialled. While he waited for the person on the other end to answer, he scanned her body and gave her a slow, knowing smile. 'I don't need to ask, *theé mou*,' he said softly. 'I already know your size.'

CHAPTER TWO

NIK LOUNGED IN his seat while the car negotiated heavy evening traffic. Beside him Lily was wriggling like a fish dropped onto the deck of a boat.

'Mr Zervakis? This dress is far more revealing than anything I would normally wear. And I've had a horrible thought.' Her voice was breathy and distracting and Nik turned his head to look at her, trying to remind himself that girls with sweet smiles who were self-confessed members of Loveaholics Anonymous were definitely off his list.

'Call me Nik.'

'I can't call you Nik. It would feel wrong while I'm working in your company. You pay my salary.'

'I pay you? I thought you said you were an intern.'

'I am. You pay your interns far more than most companies, but that's a different conversation. I'm still having that horrible thought by the way.'

Nik dragged his eyes from her mouth and tried

to wipe his brain of X-rated thoughts. 'What horrible thought is that?'

'The one where your girlfriend finds out you took me as your date tonight.'

'She will find out.'

'And that doesn't bother you?'

'Why would it?'

'Isn't it obvious? Because she didn't believe I was the cleaner. She thought you and I—well…' she turned scarlet '…if she finds out we were together tonight then it will look as if she was right and we were lying, even though if people used their brains they could work out that if she's your type then I couldn't possibly be.'

Nik tried to decipher that tumbled speech. 'You're concerned she will think we're having sex? Why is that a horrible thought? You find me unattractive?'

'That's a ridiculous question.' Lily's eyes flew to his and then away again. 'Sorry, but that's like asking a woman if she likes chocolate.'

'There are women who don't like chocolate.'

'They're lying. They might not eat it, but that doesn't mean they don't like it.'

'So I'm chocolate?' Nik tried to remember the last time he'd been this entertained by anyone.

'If you're asking if I think you're very tempting and definitely bad for me, the answer is yes. But apart from the fact we're totally unsuited, I wouldn't be able to relax enough to have sex with you.'

Nik, who had never had trouble helping a woman relax, rose to the challenge. 'I'm happy to—'

'No.' She gave him a stern look. 'I know you're competitive, but forget it. I saw that photo of you in the swimming pool. No way could I ever be naked in front of a man with a body like yours. I'd have to suck everything in and make sure you only saw my good side. The stress would kill any passion.'

'I've already seen you in your underwear.'

'Don't remind me.'

Nik caught his driver's amused gaze in the mirror and gave him a steady stare. Vassilis had been with him for over a decade and had a tendency to voice his opinions on Nik's love life. It was obvious he thoroughly approved of Lily.

'It's true that if you turn up as my guest tonight there will be people who assume we are having sex.' Nik returned his attention to the conversation. 'I can't claim to be intimately acquainted with the guest list, but I'm assuming a few of the people there will be your colleagues. Does that bother you?'

'No. It will send a message that I'm not broken-hearted, which is good for my pride. In fact the timing is perfect. Just this morning I embarked on a new project. Operation Ice Maiden. You're probably wondering what that is.'

Nik opened his mouth to comment but she carried on without pausing.

'I am going to have sex with no emotion. That's right.' She nodded at him. 'You heard me correctly. Rebound sex. I am going to climb into bed with some guy and I'm not going to feel a thing.'

Hearing a sound from the front of the car, Nik pressed a button and closed the screen between him and Vassilis, giving them privacy.

'Do you have anyone in mind for—er—Operation Ice Maiden?'

'Not yet, but if they happen to think it's you that's fine. You'd look good on my romantic résumé.'

Nik leaned his head back against the seat and started to laugh. 'You, Lily, are priceless.'

'That doesn't sound like a compliment.' She adjusted the neckline of her dress and her breasts almost escaped in the process. 'You're basically saying I'm not worth anything.'

Dragging his gaze from her body, Nik decided this was the most entertaining evening he'd had in a long time.

'There are photographers.' As they pulled up outside the museum Lily slunk lower in her seat and Nik closed his hand around her wrist and hauled her upright again.

'You look stunning. If you don't want them all surmising that we climbed out of bed to come here then you need to stop looking guilty.'

'I saw several TV cameras.'

'The opening of a new wing of the museum is news.'

'The neckline of this dress might also be news.' She tugged at it. 'My breasts are too big for this plunging style. Can I borrow your jacket?'

'Your breasts deserve a dress like that and no, you may not borrow my jacket.' His voice was a deep, masculine purr and she felt the sizzle of sexual attraction right through her body.

'Are you flirting with me?' He was completely different from the safe, friendly men who formed part of her social circle. There was a brutal strength to him, a confidence and assurance that suggested he'd never met a man he hadn't been able to beat in a fight, whether in the bar or the boardroom.

Her question appeared to amuse him. 'You're my date. Flirting is mandatory.'

'It unsettles me and I'm already unsettled at the thought of tonight.'

'Because you're with me?'

No way was she confessing how being with him really made her feel. 'No, because the opening of this new museum wing is a really momentous occasion.'

'You and I have a very different idea of what constitutes a momentous occasion, Lily.' There was laughter in his eyes. 'Never before has my ego been so effectively crushed.'

'Your ego is armour plated, like your feelings.'

'It's true that my feelings of self-worth are not dependent on the opinion of others.'

'Because you think you're right and everyone else is wrong. I wish I were more like you. What if the reporters ask who I am? What do I say? I'm a fake.'

'You're the archaeologist. I'm the fake. And you say whatever you want to say. Or say nothing.

Your decision. You're the one in charge of your mouth.'

'You have no idea how much I wish that was true.'

'Tell me why you're excited about tonight.'

'You mean apart from the fact I get to dress up? The new wing houses the biggest collection of Minoan antiquities anywhere in Greece. It has a high percentage of provenanced material, which means archaeologists will be able to restudy material from old excavations. It's exciting. And I love the dress by the way, even though I'll never have any reason to wear it again.'

'Chipped pots excite you?'

She winced. 'Don't say that on camera. The collection will play an active role in research and in university teaching as well as offering a unique insight for the general public.'

As the car pulled up outside the museum one of Nik's security team opened the door and Lily emerged to what felt like a million camera flashes.

'Unreal,' she muttered. 'Now I know why celebrities wear sunglasses.'

'Mr Zervakis—' Photographers and reporters gathered as close as they could. 'Do you have a statement about the new wing?'

Nik paused and spoke directly to the camera,

relaxed and at ease as he repeated Lily's words without a single error.

She stared at him. 'You must have an incredible short-term memory.'

A reporter stepped forward. 'Who's your guest tonight, Nik?'

Nik turned towards her and she realised he was leaving it up to her to decide whether to give them a name or not.

'I'm a friend,' she muttered and Nik smiled, took her hand and led her up the steps to the welcome committee at the top.

The first person she spotted was David Ashurst and she stopped in dismay. In answer to Nik's questioning look, she shook her head quickly, misery and panic creating a sick cocktail inside her. 'I'm fine. I saw someone I didn't expect to see, that's all. I didn't think he'd have the nerve to show up.'

'That's him?' His gaze travelled from her face to the man looking awkward at the top of the steps. 'He is the reason you're hoping for a personality transplant?'

'His name is Professor Ashurst. He has a *wife*,' she muttered in an undertone. 'Can you believe that? I actually cried over that loser. Do I have time to get my notebook out of my bag? I can't remember what I wrote down.'

'I'll tell you what to say.' He leaned closer and whispered something in her ear that made her gasp.

'I can't say that.'

'No? Then how's this for an alternative?' Sliding his arm round her waist, he pressed his hand to the base of her spine and flattened her against him. She looked up at him, hypnotised by those spectacular dark eyes and the raw sexuality in his gaze. Before she could ask what he was doing he lowered his head and kissed her.

Pleasure screamed through her, sensation scorching her skin and stoking a pool of heat low in her belly. She'd been kissed before, but never like this. Nik used his mouth with slow, sensual expertise and she felt a rush of exquisite excitement burn through her body. Her nerve endings tingled, her tummy flipped like a gymnast in a competition, and Lily was possessed by a deep, dark craving that was entirely new to her. Oblivious to their audience, she pushed against his hard, powerful frame and felt his arms tighten around her in a gesture that was unmistakably possessive. It was a taste rather than a feast, but it left her starving for more so that when he slowly lifted his head she swayed towards him dizzily, trying to balance herself.

'Wh-why did you do that?'

He dragged his thumb slowly across her lower lip and released her. 'Because you didn't know what to say and sometimes actions speak louder than words.'

'You're an amazing kisser.' Lily blinked as a flashbulb went off in her face. 'Now there's *no* chance your girlfriend will believe I'm the cleaner.'

'No chance.' His gaze lingered on her mouth. 'And she isn't my girlfriend.'

Her head spun and her legs felt shaky. She was aware of the women staring at her enviously and David gaping at her, shell-shocked.

As she floated up the last few steps to the top she smiled at him, feeling strong for the first time in days. 'Hi, Professor Ass—Ashurst.' She told herself it was the heat that was making her dizzy and disorientated, not the kiss. 'Have a safe flight home tomorrow. I'm sure your family has missed you.'

There was no opportunity for him to respond because the curator of the museum stepped forward to welcome them, shaking Nik's hand and virtually prostrating himself in gratitude.

'Mr Zervakis—your generosity—this wing is the most exciting moment of my career—' the normally articulate man was stammering. 'I know your schedule is demanding but we'd be honoured if you'd meet the team and then take a quick tour.'

Lily kept a discreet distance but Nik took her hand and clamped her next to his side, a gesture that earned her a quizzical look from Brittany, who was looking sleek and pretty in a short blue dress that showed off her long legs. She was standing next to Spy, whose eyes were glued to Lily's cleavage, confirming all her worst fears about the suitability of the dress.

The whole situation felt surreal.

One moment she'd been half naked and shivering on the bathroom floor, the next she'd been whisked into an elegant bedroom by a team of four people who had proceeded to style her hair, do her make-up and generally make her fit to be seen on the arm of Nik Zervakis.

Three dresses had magically appeared and Nik had strolled into the room in mid phone call, gestured to one of them and then left without even pausing in his conversation.

It had been on the tip of Lily's tongue to select a different dress on principle. Then she'd reasoned that not only had he provided the dress, thus allowing her to turn up at the museum opening in the first place, but that he'd picked the dress she would have chosen herself.

All the same, she felt self-conscious as her friends and colleagues working on the project at Aptera stood together while she was treated like a VIP.

As the curator led them towards the first display Lily forgot to be self-conscious and examined the pot.

'This is early Minoan.'

Nik stared at it with a neutral expression. 'You know that because it's more cracked than the others?'

'No. Because their ceramics were characterised by linear patterns. Look—' She took his arm and drew him closer to the glass. 'Spirals, crosses, triangles, curved lines—' She talked to him about each one and he listened carefully before strolling further along the glass display cabinet.

'This one has a bird.'

'Naturalistic designs were characteristic of the Middle Minoan period. The sequencing of ceramic styles has helped archaeologists define the three phases of Minoan culture.'

He stared down in her eyes. 'Fascinating.'

Her heart bumped hard against her chest and

as the curator moved away to answer questions from the press she stepped closer to him. 'You're not really fascinated, are you?'

'I am.' His eyes dropped to her mouth with blatant interest. 'But I think it might be because you're the one saying it. I love the way you get excited about things that put other people to sleep, and your mouth looks cute when you say "Minoan". It makes you pout.'

She tried not to laugh. 'You're impossible. To you it's an old pot, but it can have tremendous significance. Ceramics help archaeologists establish settlement and trading patterns. We can reconstruct human activity based on the distribution of pottery. It gives us an idea of population size and social complexity. Why are you donating so much money to the museum if it isn't an interest of yours?'

'Because I'm interested in preserving Greek culture. I donate the money. It's up to them to decide how to use it. I don't micromanage and gifts don't come with strings.'

'Why didn't you insist that it was called "The Zervakis Wing" or something? Most benefactors want their name in the title.'

'It's about preserving history, not about advertising my name.' His eyes gleamed. 'And ZervaCo is a modern, forward-thinking company at the cutting edge of technology development. I don't want the name associated with a museum.'

'You're joking.'

'Yes, I'm joking.' His smile faded as Spy and Brittany joined them.

'They're good friends of mine,' Lily said quickly, 'so you can switch off the full-wattage intimidation.'

'If you're sure.' He introduced himself to both of them and chatted easily with Spy while Brittany pulled Lily to one side.

'I don't even know where to start with my questions.'

'Probably just as well because I wouldn't know where to start with my answers.'

'I'm guessing he's the owner of Villa You-Have-to-be-Kidding-Me.'

'He is.'

'I'm not going to ask,' Brittany muttered and then grinned. 'Oh hell, yes I am. I'm asking. What happened? He found you in the cellar fighting off the ugly sisters and decided to bring you to the ball?'

'Close. He found me on the floor of his bathroom where I'd been attacked and left for dead by his power shower. After I broke up his relationship, he needed a replacement and I was the only person around.'

Brittany started to laugh. 'You were left for dead by his power shower?'

'You said you wouldn't ask.'

'These things only ever happen to you, Lily.'

'I am aware of that. I am really not good with technology.'

'Maybe not, but you know how to pick your rebound guy. He is spectacular. And you look stunning.' Brittany's curious gaze slid over her from head to foot. 'It's a step up from dusty shorts and hiking boots.'

Lily frowned. 'He isn't my rebound guy.'

'Why not? He is smoking hot. And there's something about him.' Her friend narrowed her eyes as she scanned Nik's broad shoulders and powerful frame. 'A suggestion of the uncivilised under the civilised, if you know what I mean.' Brittany put her hand on her arm and her voice was suddenly serious. 'Be careful.'

'Why would I need to be careful? I'm never setting foot in his shower again, if that's what you mean.'

'It isn't what I mean. That man is not tame.'

'He's surprisingly amusing company.'

'That makes him even more dangerous. He's a

tiger, not a pussycat and he hasn't taken his eyes off you for five seconds. I don't want to see you hurt again.'

'I have never been in less danger of being hurt. He isn't my type.'

Brittany looked at her. 'Nik Zervakis is the man equivalent of Blood Type O. He is everyone's type.'

'Not mine.'

'He kissed you,' Brittany said dryly, 'so I'm guessing he might have a different opinion on that.'

'He kissed me because I didn't know what to say to David. I was in an awkward position and he helped me out. He did that for me.'

'Lily, a guy like him does things for himself. Don't make a mistake about that. He does what he wants, with whoever he wants to do it, at a time that suits him.'

'I know. Don't worry about me.' Smiling at Brittany, she moved back to Nik. 'Looks like the party is breaking up. Thanks for a fun evening. I'll post you the dress back and any time you need your shower cleaned let me know. I owe you.'

He stared down at her for a long moment, ignoring everyone around them. 'Have dinner with me. I have a reservation at The Athena at nine.'

She'd heard of The Athena. Who hadn't? It was one of the most celebrated restaurants in the whole of Greece. Eating there was a once-in-a-lifetime experience for most people and a never-in-this-lifetime experience for her.

Those incredible dark eyes held hers and Brittany's voice flitted into her head.

He's a tiger, not a pussycat.

From the way he was looking at her mouth, she wondered if he intended her to be the guest or the meal.

'That's a joke, right?' She gave a half-smile and looked away briefly, awkward, out of her depth. When she looked back at him she was still the only one smiling.

'I never joke about food.'

Something curled low in her stomach. 'Nik...' she spoke softly '...this has been amazing. Really out of this world and something to tell my kids one day, but you're a gazillionaire and I'm a—a—'

'Sexy woman who looks great in that dress.'

There was something about him that made her feel as if she were floating two feet above the ground.

'I was going to say I'm a dusty archaeologist

who can't even figure out how to use your power shower.'

'I'll teach you. Have dinner with me, Lily.' His soft command made her wonder if anyone had ever said no to him.

Thrown by the look in his eyes and the almost unbearable sexual tension, she was tempted. Then she remembered her rule about never dating anyone who didn't fit her basic criteria. 'I can't. But I'll never forget this evening. Thank you.' Because she was afraid she'd change her mind, she turned and walked quickly towards the exit.

What a crazy day it had been.

Part of her was longing to look back, to see if he was watching her.

Of course he wouldn't be watching her. Look at how quickly he'd replaced Christina. Within two minutes of her refusal, Nik Zervakis would be inviting someone else to dinner.

David stood in the doorway, blocking her exit. 'What are you doing with him?'

'None of your business.'

His jaw tightened. 'Did you kiss him to make me jealous or to help you get over me?'

'I kissed him because he's a hot guy, and I was over you the moment I found out you were married.' Realising it was true, Lily felt a rush of relief but that relief was tempered by the knowledge that her system for evaluating prospective life partners was seriously flawed.

'I know you love me.'

'You're wrong. And if you really knew me, you'd know I'm incapable of loving a man who is married to another woman.' Her voice and hands were shaking. 'You have a wife. A family.'

'I'll work something out.'

'Did you really just say that to me?' Lily stared at him, appalled. 'A family is *not* disposable. You don't come and go as it suits you, nor do you "work something out". You stick by them through thick and thin.' Disgusted and disillusioned, she tried to step past him but he caught her arm.

'You don't understand. Things are tough right now.'

'I don't care.' She dug her fingers into clammy palms. Knowing that her response was deeply personal, she looked away. 'A real man doesn't walk away when things get tough.'

'You're forgetting how good it was between us.'

'And you're forgetting the promises you made.' She dragged her arm out of his grip. 'Go back to your wife.'

He glanced over her shoulder towards Nik. 'I never thought you were the sort to be turned on by money, but obviously I was wrong. I hope you know what you're doing because all that man will ever give you is one night. A man like him is only interested in sex.'

'What did you say?' Lily stared at him and then turned her head to look at Nik. The sick feeling in her stomach eased and her spirits lifted. 'You're right. Thank you so much.'

'For making you realise he's wrong for you?'

'For making me realise he's perfect. Now stop looking down the front of my dress and go home to your wife and kids.' With that, she stalked past him and spotted the reporter who had asked her identity on the way in. 'Lily,' she said clearly. 'Lily Rose. That's my name. And yes, Rose is my second name.'

Then she turned and stalked back into the museum, straight up to Nik, who was deep in conversation with two important-looking men in suits.

All talk ceased as Lily walked up to him, her heels making the same rhythmic tapping sound that Christina's had earlier in the evening. She decided heels were her new favourite thing for illustrating mood. 'What time is that restaurant reservation?'

He didn't miss a beat. 'Nine o'clock.'

'Then we should leave, because we don't want

to be late.' She stood on tiptoe and planted a kiss firmly on his mouth. 'And just so that you know, whatever you're planning on doing with the dress, I'm keeping the shoes.'

CHAPTER THREE

THE ATHENA WAS situated on the edge of town, on a hill overlooking Souda Bay with the White Mountains dominating the horizon behind them.

Still on a high after her confrontation with David, Lily sailed into the restaurant feeling like royalty. 'You have no idea how good it felt to tell David to go home to his wife. I felt like punching the air. You see what a few hours in your company has done for me? I'm already transformed. Your icy control and lack of emotional engagement is contagious.'

Nik guided her to his favourite table, tucked away behind a discreet screen of vines. 'You certainly showed the guy what he was missing.'

Lily frowned. 'I didn't want to show him what he was missing. I wanted him to learn a lesson and never lie or cheat again. I wanted him to think of his poor wife. Marriage should be for ever. No cheating. Mess around as much as you like before if that's what you want, but once you've made that commitment, that's it. Don't you agree?'

'Definitely. Which is why I've never made that commitment,' he said dryly. 'I'm still at the "messing around" stage and I expect to stay firmly trapped in that stage for the rest of my life.'

'You don't want a family? We're very different. It's brilliant.' She smiled at him and his eyes narrowed.

'Why is that brilliant?'

'Because you're completely and utterly wrong for me. We don't want the same things.'

'I'm relieved to hear it.' He leaned back in his chair. 'I hardly dare ask what you want.'

She hesitated. 'Someone like you will think I'm a ridiculous romantic.'

'Tell me.'

She dragged her gaze from his and looked over the tumbling bougainvillea to the sea beyond. *Was she a ridiculous romantic?*

Was she setting herself unachievable goals?

Seduced by the warmth of his gaze and the beauty of the spectacular sunset, she told the truth. 'I want the whole fairy tale.'

'Which fairy tale? The one where the stepmother

poisons the apple or the one where the prince has to deal with a heroine with narcolepsy?'

She laughed. 'The happy-ending part. I want to fall in love, settle down and have lots of babies.' Enjoying herself, she looked him in the eye. 'Am I freaking you out yet?'

'That depends. Are you expecting to do any of that with me?'

'No! Of course not.'

'Then you're not freaking me out.'

'I start every relationship in the genuine belief it might go somewhere.'

'I presume you mean somewhere other than bed?'

'I do. I have never been interested in sex for the sake of sex.'

Nik looked amused. 'That's the only sort of sex I'm interested in.'

She sat back in her chair and looked at him. 'I've never had sex with a man I wasn't in love with. I fall in love, then I have sex. I think sex cements my emotional connection to someone.' She sneaked another look at him. 'You don't have that problem, do you?'

'I'm not looking for an emotional connection, if that's what you're asking.'

'I want to be more like you. I decided this morning I'm going to have cold, emotionless rebound sex. I'm switching everything off. It's going to be wham, bam, thank you, man.'

The corners of his mouth flickered. 'Do you have anyone in mind for this project?'

She sensed this wasn't the moment to confess he was right at the top of her list. 'I'm going to pick a guy I couldn't possibly fall in love with. Then I'll be safe. It will be like—' she struggled to find the right description '—emotional contraception. I'll be taking precautions. Wearing a giant condom over my feelings. Protecting myself. I bet you do that all the time.'

'If you're asking if I've ever pulled a giant condom over my feelings, the answer is no.'

'You're laughing at me, but if you'd been hurt as many times as I have you wouldn't be laughing. So if emotions don't play a part in your relationships, what exactly is sex to you?'

'Recreation.' He took a menu from the waiter and she felt a rush of mortification. As soon as he walked away, she gave a groan.

'How long had he been standing there?'

'Long enough to know you're planning on having cold, unemotional rebound sex and that you're thinking of wearing a giant condom over your feelings. I think that was the point he decided it was time to take our order.'

She covered her face with her hands. 'We need to leave. I'm sure the food here is delicious, but we need to eat somewhere different or I need to take my plate under the table.'

'You're doing it again. Letting emotions govern your actions.'

'But he *heard* me. Aren't you embarrassed?'

'Why would I be embarrassed?'

'Aren't you worried about what he might think of you?'

'Why would I care what he thinks? I don't know him. His role is to serve our food and make sure we enjoy ourselves sufficiently to want to come back. His opinion on anything else is irrelevant. Carry on with what you were saying. It was fascinating. Dining with you is like learning about an alien species. You were telling me you're going to pick a guy you can't fall in love with and use him for sex.'

'And you were telling me sex is recreation—like football?'

'No, because football is a group activity. I'm possessive, so for me it's strictly one on one.'

Her heart gave a little flip. 'That sounds like a type of commitment.'

'I'm one hundred per cent committed for the time a woman is in my bed. She is the sole focus of my attention.'

Her stomach uncurled with a slow, dangerous heat. 'But that might only be for a night?'

He simply smiled and she leaned back with a shocked laugh.

'You are so *bad*. And honest. I love that.'

'As long as you don't love *me*, we don't have a problem.'

'I could never love you. You are so wrong for me.'

'I think we should drink to that.' He raised a hand and moments later champagne appeared on the table.

'I can't believe you live like this. A driver, bottles of champagne—' She lifted the glass, watching the bubbles. 'Your villa is bigger than quite a few Greek islands and there is only one of you.'

'I like space and light and property is always a good investment.' He handed the menu back to the waiter. 'Is there any food you don't eat?'

'I eat everything.' She paused while he spoke to the waiter in Greek. 'Are you seriously ordering for me?'

'The menu is in Greek and you were talking about sex so I was aiming to keep the interaction as brief as possible in order to prevent you from feeling the need to dine under the table.'

'In that case I'll forgive you.' She waited until the waiter had walked away with their order. 'So if property is an investment that means you'd *sell* your home?'

'I have four homes.'

Her jaw dropped. 'Four? Why does one person need four homes? One for every season or something?'

'I have offices in New York, San Francisco and London and I don't like staying in hotels.'

'So you buy a house. That is the rich man's way of solving a problem. Which one do you think of as home?' Seeing the puzzled look on his face, she elaborated. 'Where do your family live? Do you have family? Are your parents alive?'

'They are.'

'Happily married?'

'Miserably divorced. In my father's case three times so far, but he's always in competition with himself so I'm expecting a fourth as soon as the wedding is out of the way.'

'And your mother?' She saw a faint shift in his expression.

'My mother is American. She lives in Boston with her third husband who is a divorce lawyer.'

'So do you think of yourself as Greek American or American Greek?'

He gave a careless lift of his broad shoulders. 'Whichever serves my purpose at the time.'

'Wow. So you have this big, crazy family.' Lily felt a flash of envy. 'That must be wonderful.'

'Why?'

'You don't think it's wonderful? I guess we never appreciate something when we have it.' She said it lightly but felt his dark gaze fix on her across the table.

'Are you going to cry?'

'No, of course not.'

'Good. Because tears are the one form of emotional expression I don't tolerate.'

She stole an olive from the bowl on the table. 'What if someone is upset?'

'Then they need to walk away from me until they've sorted themselves out, or be prepared for me to walk away. I never allow myself to be manipulated and ninety-nine per cent of tears are manipulation.'

'What about the one per cent which are an expression of genuine emotion?'

'I've never encountered that rare beast, so I'm willing to play the odds.'

'If that's your experience, you must have met

some awful women in your time. I don't believe you'd be that unsympathetic.'

'Believe it.' He leaned back as the waiter delivered a selection of dishes. 'These are Cretan specialities. Try them.' He spooned beans in a rich tomato sauce onto her plate and added local goat's cheese.

She nibbled the beans and moaned with pleasure. 'These are delicious. I still can't believe you ordered for me. Do you want to feed me, too? Because I could lie back and let you drop grapes into my mouth if that would be fun. Or you could cover my naked body with whipped cream. Is that the sort of stuff you do in bed?'

There was a dangerous glitter in his eyes. 'You don't want to know the sort of "stuff" I do in bed, Lily. You're far too innocent.'

She remembered what Brittany had said about him not being tame. 'I'm not innocent. I have big eyes and that gives people a false impression of me.'

'You remind me of a kitten that's been abandoned by the side of the road.'

'You've got me totally wrong. I'd say I'm more of a panther.' She clawed the air and growled. 'A little bit predatory. A little bit dangerous.'

He gave her a long steady look and she blushed and lowered her hand.

'All right, maybe not a *panther* exactly but not a kitten either.' She thought about what lay in her past. 'I'll have you know I'm pretty tough. Tell me more about your family. So you have a father and a few stepmothers. How about siblings?'

'I have one half-sister who is two.'

Lily softened. 'I love that age. They're so busy and into everything. Is she adorable?'

'I've no idea. I've never met her.'

'You've—' She stared at him, shocked. 'You mean it's been a while since you've seen her.'

'No. I mean I've never seen her.' He lifted his champagne. 'Her mother extracted all the money she could from my father and then left. She lives in Athens and visits when she wants something.'

'Oh, my God, that's *terrible*.' Lily's eyes filled. 'Your poor, poor father.'

He put his glass down slowly. 'Are you crying for my father?'

'No.' Her throat was thickened. 'Maybe. Yes, a little bit.'

'A man you've never met and know nothing about.'

'Maybe I'm the one per cent who cares.' She sniffed and he shook his head in exasperation.

'This is your tough, ruthless streak? How can you be sad for someone you don't know?'

'Because I sympathise with his situation. He doesn't see his little girl and that must be so hard. Family is the most important thing in the world and it is often the least appreciated thing.'

'If you let a single tear fall onto your cheek,' he said softly, 'I'm walking out of here.'

'I don't believe you. You wouldn't be that heartless. I think it's all a big act you put on to stop women slobbering all over you.'

'Do you want to test it?' His tone was cool. 'Because I suggest you wait until the end of the meal. The lamb *kleftiko* is the best anywhere in Greece and they make a house special with honey and pistachio nuts that you wouldn't want to miss.'

'But if you're the one walking out, then I can stay here and eat your portion.' She helped herself to another spoonful of food from the dish closest to her. 'I don't know why you're so freaked out by tears. It's not as if I was expecting you to hug me. I've taught myself to self-soothe.'

'Self-soothe?' Some of the tension left him. 'You hug yourself?'

'It's important to be independent.' She'd been self-sufficient from an early age, but the ability to do everything for herself hadn't removed the deep longing to share her life with someone. 'Why did your dad and his last wife divorce?'

'Because they married,' he said smoothly, 'and divorce is an inevitable consequence of marriage.'

She wondered why he had such a grim view of marriage. 'Not all marriages.'

'All but those infected with extreme inertia.'

'So you're saying that even people who stay married would divorce if they could be bothered to make the effort.'

'I think there are any number of reasons for a couple to stay together, but love isn't one of them. In my father's case, wife number three married him for his money and the novelty wore off.'

'Does "wife number three" have a name?'

'Callie.' His hard tone told her everything she needed to know about his relationship with his last stepmother.

'You don't like her?'

'Are you enjoying your meal?'

She blinked, thrown by the change of subject. 'It's delicious, but—'

'Good. If you're hoping to sample dessert, you need to talk about something other than my family.'

'You control everything, even the conversation.'

She wondered why he didn't want to talk about his family. 'Is this where you bring all the women you date?'

'It depends on the woman.'

'How about that woman you were with earlier—Christina? She definitely wouldn't have eaten any of this. She had carb-phobia written all over her.'

Those powerful shoulders relaxed slightly. 'She would have ordered green salad, grilled fish and eaten half of it.'

'So why didn't you order green salad and grilled fish for me?'

'Because you look like someone who enjoys food.'

Lily gave him a look. 'I'm starting to understand why women cry around you. You basically called me fat. For your information, most women would storm out if you said that to them.'

'So why didn't you storm out?'

'Because eating here is a once-in-a-lifetime experience and I don't want to miss it. And I don't think you meant it that way and I like to give people the benefit of the doubt. Tell me what happens next on a date. You bring a woman to a place like this and then you take her back to your villa for sex in that massive bed?'

'I never talk about my relationships.'

'You don't talk about your family and you don't talk about your relationships.' Lily helped herself to rich, plump slices of tomato salad. 'What do you want to talk about?'

'You. Tell me about your work.'

'I work in your company. You know more about what goes on than I do, but one thing I will say is that with all these technology skills at your disposal you need to invent an app that syncs all the details of the women who call you. You have a busy sex life and it's easy to get it mixed up, especially as they're all pretty much the same type.' She put her fork down. 'Is that the secret to staying emotionally detached? You date women who are clones, no individual characteristics to tell them apart.'

'I do not date clones, and I don't want to talk about my work, I want to talk about your work. Your archaeological work.' His eyes gleamed. 'And try to include the word "Minoan" at least eight times in each sentence.'

She ignored that. 'I'm a ceramics expert. I did a masters in archaeology and since then I've been working on an internationally funded project replicating Minoan cooking fabrics. Among other things we've been looking at the technological shift Minoan potters made when they replaced hand-building methods with the wheel. We can trace patterns of production, but also the context of ceramic consumption. The word ceramic comes from the Greek, *keramikos,* but you probably already know that.'

He reached for his wine glass. 'I can't believe you were cleaning my shower.'

'Cleaning your shower pays well and I have college debts.'

'If you didn't have college debts, what would you be doing?'

She hesitated, unwilling to share her dream with a stranger, especially one who couldn't possibly understand having to make choices driven by debt. 'I have no idea. I can't afford to think like that. I have to be practical.'

'Why Crete?'

'Crete had all the resources necessary to produce pottery. Clay, temper, water and fuel. Microscopic ceramic fabric analysis indicate those resources have been used for at least eight thousand years. The most practical way of understanding ancient technology is to replicate it and use it and that's what we've been doing.'

'So you've been trying to cook like a Minoan?'

'Yes. We're using tools and materials that would have been available during the Cretan Bronze Age.'

'That's what you're digging for?'

'Brittany and the team have different objectives, but while they're digging I'm able to access clay. I spend some of my time on site and some of my time at the museum with a small team, but that's all coming to an end now. Tell me what you do.'

'You work in my company. You should know what I do.'

'I don't know *specifically* what you do. I know you're a technology wizard. I guess that's why you have a shower that looks like something from NASA. I bet you're good with computers. Technology isn't really my thing, but you probably already know that.'

'If technology isn't your thing, why are you working in my company?'

'I'm not dealing with the technology side. I'm dealing with people. I did a short spell in Human Resources—you keep them busy by the way—and now I'm working with your personal assistants. I still haven't decided what I want to do with my life so I'm trying different things. It's only two days a week and I wanted to see how I enjoyed corporate life.'

'And how are you enjoying "corporate life"?'

'It's different.' She dodged the question and he gave her a long, speculative look.

'Tell me why you became involved with that guy who looked old enough to be your father.'

Her stomach lurched. *Because she was an idiot.* 'I never talk about my relationships.'

'On short acquaintance I'd say the problem is stopping you talking, not getting you talking. Tell me.' Something about that compelling dark gaze made it impossible not to confide.

'I think I was attracted to his status and gravitas. I was flattered when he paid me attention. A psychologist would probably say it has something to do with not having a father around when I was growing up. Anyway, he pursued me pretty heavily and it got serious fast. And then I found out he was married.' She lowered her voice and pulled a face. 'I hate myself for that, but most of all I hate him for lying to me.' Knowing his views on marriage, she wondered if he'd think she was ridiculously principled but his eyes were hard.

'You cried over this guy?'

'I think perhaps I was crying because history repeated itself. My relationships always follow the same pattern. I meet someone I'm attracted to, he's caring, attentive and a really good listener—

I fall in love, have sex with him, start planning a future and then suddenly that's it. We break up.'

'And this experience hasn't put you off love?'

Perhaps it should have done.

No one had ever stayed in her life.

From an early age she'd wondered what it was about her that made it so easy for people to walk away.

The dishes were cleared away and a sticky, indulgent dessert placed in the centre of the table.

She tried to pull herself together. 'If you have one bad meal you don't stop eating, do you? And by the way this is the best meal I've ever had in my whole life.' She stuck her spoon in the pastry and honey oozed over the plate. She decided this was the perfect time to check a few facts before finally committing herself. 'Tell me what happens in your relationships. We'll talk hypothetically as you don't like revealing specifics. Let's say you meet a woman and you find her attractive. What happens next?'

'I take her on a date.'

'What sort of date?' Lily licked the spoon. 'Dinner? Theatre? Movie? Walk on the beach?'

'Any of those.'

'Let's say it's dinner. What would you talk about?'

'Anything.'

'Anything as long as it isn't to do with your family or relationships.'

He smiled. 'Exactly.'

'So you talk, you drink expensive wine, you admire the romantic view—then what? You take her home or you take her to bed?'

'Yes.' He paused as their waiter delivered a bottle of clear liquid and two glasses and Lily shook her head.

'Is that raki? Brittany loves it, but it gives me a headache.'

'We call it *tsikoudia*. It is a grape liqueur—an important part of Cretan hospitality.'

'I know. It's been around since Minoan times. Archaeologists have found the petrified remains of grapes and grape pips inside *pithoi*, the old clay storage jars, so it's assumed they knew plenty about distillation. Doesn't change the fact it gives me a headache.'

'Then you didn't drink it with enough water.' He handed her a small glass. 'The locals think it promotes a long and healthy life.'

Lily took a sip and felt her throat catch fire as she swallowed. 'So now finish telling me about your typical date. You don't fall in love, because you don't believe in love. So when you take a woman to bed, there are no feelings involved at all?'

'There are plenty of feelings involved.' The look he gave her made her heart pump faster.

'I mean emotions. You have emotionless sex. You don't say *I love you*. You don't feel anything here—' Lily put her hand on her heart. 'No feelings. So it's all about physical satisfaction. This is basically a naked workout, yes? It's like a bench press for two.'

'Sex may not be emotional, but it's intimate,' he said softly. 'It requires the ultimate degree of trust.'

'You can do that and still not be emotionally involved?'

'When I'm with a woman I care about her enjoyment, her pleasure, her happiness and her comfort. I don't love her.'

'You don't love women?'

'I do love women.' The corners of his mouth flickered. 'I just don't want to love one specific woman.'

Lily stared at him in fascination.

There was no way, *no way*, she would ever fall in love with a man like Nik. She didn't even need to check her list to know he didn't tick a single one of the boxes.

He was perfect.

'There's something I want to say to you and I hope you're not going to be shocked.' She put her glass down and took a deep breath. 'I want to have rebound sex. No emotions involved. Sex without falling in love. Not something I've ever done before, so this is all new to me.'

He watched her from under lowered lids, his expression unreadable. There was a dangerous stillness about him. 'And you're telling me this because—?'

'Because you seem to be the expert.' Her heart started to pound. 'I want you to take me to bed.'

CHAPTER FOUR

NIK SCANNED HER in silence. The irony was that his original plan had been to do exactly that. Take her to bed. She was fun, sexy and original but the longer he spent in her company the more he realised how different her life goals were from his own. By her own admittance, Lily wasn't the sort to emotionally disengage in a relationship. In the interests of self-protection, logic took precedence over his libido.

'It's time I took you home.'

Far from squashing her, the news appeared to cheer her. 'That's what I was hoping you'd say. I promise you won't regret it. What I lack in experience I make up for in enthusiasm.'

She was as bright as she was pretty and he knew her 'misunderstanding' was deliberate.

'*Theé mou*, you should *not* be saying things like that to a man. It could be taken the wrong way.'

She sliced into a tomato. 'You're taking it the way I intended you to take it.'

Nik glanced at the bottle of champagne and tried to work out how much she'd had. 'I'm not taking you to my home, I'm taking you to *your* home.'

'You don't want to do that. My bed is smaller than a cat basket and you're big. I have a feeling we're going to get very hot and sweaty, and I don't have air conditioning.'

Nik's libido was fighting against the restraining bonds of logic. 'I will give you a lift home and then I'm leaving.'

'Leaving?' Disappointment mingled with uncertainty. 'You don't find me attractive?'

'You're sexy as hell,' he drawled, 'but you're not my type.'

'That doesn't make any sense. You don't like sexy?'

'I like sexy. I don't like women who want to fall in love, settle down and have lots of babies.'

'I thought we'd already established I didn't want to do any of that with you. You don't score a single point on my checklist, which is *exactly* why I want to do this. I know I'd be safe. And so would you!'

He decided he didn't even want to know about her checklist. 'How much champagne have you had?'

'I'm not drunk, if that's what you're suggesting. Ask me anything. Make me walk in a straight line. I'll touch my nose with my eyes closed, or I'll touch *your* nose with my eyes closed if you prefer. Or other parts of you—' She gave a wicked grin and leaned forward. 'One night. That's all it would be. You will not regret it.'

Nik deployed the full force of his will power and kept his eyes away from the softness of her breasts. 'You're right. I won't, because it's not going to happen.'

'I do yoga. I'm very bendy.'

Nik gave a soft curse. 'Stop talking.'

'I can put my legs behind my head.'

'*Cristo*, you should *definitely* stop talking.' His libido was urging logic to surrender.

'What's the problem? One night of fun. Tomorrow we both go our own ways and if I see you in the office I'll pretend I don't know you. Call your lawyer. I'll sign a contract promising not to fall in love with you. A pre-non-nuptial agreement. All I want is for you to take me home, strip me naked, throw me onto that enormous bed of yours and have sex with me in every conceivable position. After that I will walk out of your door and you'll never see me again. Deal?'

He tried to respond but it seemed her confusing mix of innocence and sexuality had short-circuited his brain. 'Lily—' he spoke through his teeth '—trust me, you do *not* want me to take you home, strip you naked and throw you onto my bed.'

'Why not? It's just sex.'

'You've spent several hours telling me you don't do "just sex".'

'But I'm going to this time. I want to be able to separate sex from love. The next time a man comes my way who might be the one, I won't let sex confuse things. I'll be like Kevlar. Nothing is getting through me. Nothing.'

'You are marshmallow, not Kevlar.'

'That was the old me. The new me is Kevlar. I don't understand why you won't do this, un-less—' She studied him for a long moment and then leaned forward, a curious look in her eyes. 'Are you *scared*?'

'I'm sober,' he said softly, 'and when I play, I like it to be with an opponent who is similarly matched.'

'I'm tougher than I look.' A dimple appeared in the corner of her mouth. 'Drink another glass of champagne and then call Vassilis.'

'How do you know my driver's name?'

'I listen. And he has a kind face. There really is no need to be nervous. If rumour is correct, you're a cold, emotionless vacuum and that means you're in no danger from someone like little me.'

He had a feeling 'little me' was the most dangerous thing he'd encountered in a long while. 'If I'm a "cold, emotionless vacuum", why would you want to climb into my bed?'

'Because you are *insanely* sexy and all the things that make you so wrong for me would make you perfect for rebound sex.'

He looked into those blue eyes and tried to ignore the surge of sexual hunger that had gripped him from the moment he'd laid eyes on that pale silky hair tumbling damp round her gleaming wet body.

Never before had doing the right thing felt so wrong.

Nik cursed under his breath and rose to his feet. 'We're leaving.'

'Good decision.' She slid her hand into his, rose on tiptoe and whispered in his ear. 'I'll be gentle with you.'

With her wide smile and laughing eyes, it was like being on a date with a beam of sunshine. He felt heat spread through his body, his arousal so brutal he was tempted to haul her behind the nearest lockable door, rip off that dress and acquaint himself with every part of her luscious, naked body.

Vassilis was waiting outside with the car and Nik bundled her inside and sat as far from her as possible.

All his life, he'd avoided women like her. Women who believed in romance and 'the one'. For him, the myth of love had been smashed in childhood along with Santa and the Tooth Fairy. He had no use for it in his life.

'Where do you live?' He growled the words but she simply smiled.

'You don't need to know, because we're going back to your place. Your bed is almost big enough to be seen from outer space.'

Nik ran his hand over his jaw. 'Lily—'

Her phone signalled a text and she dug around in her bag. 'I need to answer this. It will be Brittany, checking I'm all right. She and Spy are probably worried because they saw me go off with you.'

'Maybe you should pay attention to your friends.'

'Hold that thought—'

Having rebound sex. She mouthed the words as she typed. Speak to you tomorrow.

Nik was tempted to seize the phone and text her

friends to come and pick her up. 'Brittany was the girl in the blue dress?'

'She's the female version of you, but without the money. She doesn't engage emotionally. I found out today that she was married for ten days when she was eighteen. Can you believe that? Ten days. I don't know the details, but apparently it cured her of ever wanting a repeat performance.' She pressed send and slid the phone back into her bag. 'I grew up in foster homes so I don't have any family. I think that's probably why my friends are so important to me. I never really had a sense of belonging anywhere. That's a very lonely feeling as a child.'

He felt something stir inside him, as if she'd poked a stick into a muddy, stagnant pool that had lain dormant and undiscovered for decades. Deeply uncomfortable, he shifted in his seat. 'Why are you telling me this?'

'I thought as we're going to have sex, you might want to know something about me.'

'I don't.'

'That's not very polite.'

'I'm not striving for "polite". This is who I am. It's not too late for my driver to drop you home. Give him the address.'

She leaned forward and pressed the button so that the screen closed between him and the driver. 'Sorry, Vassilis, but I don't want to corrupt you.' She slid across the seat, closed her eyes and lifted her face to his. 'Kiss me. Whatever it is you do, do it now.'

Nik had always considered himself to be a disciplined man but he was rapidly rethinking that assessment. With her, there was no discipline. He looked down at those long, thick eyelashes and the pink curve of her mouth and tried to remember when he'd last been tempted to have sex in the back of his car.

'No.' He managed to inject the word with forceful conviction but instead of retreating, she advanced.

'In that case I'll kiss you. I don't mind taking the initiative.' Her slim fingers slid to the inside of his thigh. He was so aroused he couldn't even remember why he was fighting this, and instead of pushing her away he gripped her hand hard and turned his head towards her.

His gaze swept her flushed cheeks and the lush curve of her mouth. With a rough curse he lowered his head, driving her lips apart with his tongue and taking that mouth in a kiss that was as rough as it was sexually explicit. His intention was to scare her off, so there was no holding back, no diluting of his passion. He kissed her hard, expecting to feel her pull back but instead she pressed closer. She tasted of sugar and sweet temptation, her mouth soft and eager against his as she all but wriggled onto his lap.

The heavy weight of her breasts brushed against his arm and he gave a groan and slid his hand into her hair, anchoring her head for the hard demands of his kiss. She licked into his mouth, snuggling closer like a kitten, those full soft curves pressing against him. It was a kiss without boundaries, an explosion of raw desire that built until the rear of the car shimmered with stifling heat and sexual awareness.

He slid his hand under her dress, over the smooth skin of her thigh to the soft shadows between her legs. It was her thickened moan of pleasure that woke him up.

Cristo, they were in the car, in moving traffic.

Releasing her as if she were a hot coal, he pushed her away. 'I thought you were supposed to be smart.'

Her breathing was shallow and rapid. 'I'm very, very smart. And you're an amazing kisser. Are you as good at everything else?'

His pulse was throbbing and he was so painfully aroused he didn't dare move. 'If you really want to come home with me then you're not as smart as you look.'

'What makes you think that?'

'Because a woman like you should steer clear of men like me. I don't have a love life, I have a sex life. I'll use you. If you're in my bed it will be all about pleasure and nothing else. I don't care about your feelings. I'm not kind. I'm not gentle. I need you to know that.'

There was a long, loaded silence and then her gaze slid to his mouth. 'Okay, I get it. No fluffy kittens in this relationship. Message received and understood. Can this car go any faster because I don't think I've ever been this turned on in my life before.'

She wasn't the only one. His self-control was stretched to breaking point. Why was he fighting it? She was an adult. She wasn't drunk and she knew what she was doing. Logic didn't just surrender to libido, it was obliterated. All the same, something made him open one more exit door. 'Be very sure, Lily.'

'I'm sure. I've never been so sure of anything in my life. Unless you want to be arrested for per-

forming an indecent act in a public place you'd
better tell Vassilis to break a few speed limits.'

Lily walked into the villa she'd cleaned earlier,
feeling ridiculously nervous. In the romantic setting of the restaurant this had seemed like a good
idea. Now she wasn't quite so sure. 'So why did
you hire a contract cleaning company?'

'I didn't.' He threw his jacket over the back of
a chair with careless disregard for its future appearance. 'I have staff who look after this place.
Presumably they arranged it. I didn't give them
much notice of my return. I don't care how they
do their job as long as it gets done.'

She paced across the living room and stared
across the floodlit shimmer of the infinity pool.
'It's pretty at night.' It was romantic, but she knew
this had nothing to do with romance. Her other
relationships had been with men she knew and
cared about. This scenario was new to her. 'Do
you have something to drink?'

'You're thirsty?'

Nervous. 'A little.'

He gave her a long look, strolled out of the room
and returned moments later carrying a glass of
water.

'I want you sober,' he said softly. 'In fact I insist on it.'

Realising they were actually going to do this, she suddenly found she was shaking so much the water sloshed out of the glass and onto the floor. 'Oops. I'm messing up the floor I cleaned earlier.'

He was standing close to her and her gaze drifted to the bronzed skin at the base of his throat and the blue-shadowed jaw. Everything about him was unapologetically masculine. He wasn't just dangerously attractive, he was lethal and suddenly she wondered what on earth she was doing. Maybe she should have taken up Spy's offer of rebound sex, except that Spy didn't induce one tenth of this crazy response in her. A thrilling sense of anticipation mingled with wicked excitement and she knew she'd regret it for ever if she walked away. She knew she took relationships too seriously. If she was going to try a different approach then there was surely no better man to do it with than Nik.

'Scared?' His voice was deep, dark velvet and she gave a smile.

'A little. But only because I don't normally do this and you're not my usual type. It's like passing your driving test and then getting behind the wheel of a Ferrari. I'm worried I'll crash you into a lamppost.' She put the glass down carefully on the glass table and ran her damp hands over her thighs. 'Okay, let's do this. Ignore the fact I'm shaking, go right ahead and do your bad, bad thing, whatever that is.'

He said nothing. Just looked at her, that dark gaze uncomfortably penetrating.

She waited, heart pounding, virtually squirming on the spot. 'I'm not good with delayed gratification. I'm more of an instant person. I like to—'

'Hush.' Finally he spoke and then he reached out and drew her against him, the look in his eyes driving words and thoughts from her head. She felt the warmth of his hand against the base of her spine, the slow, sensitive stroke of his fingers low on her back and then he lifted his hands and cupped her face, forcing her to look at him. 'Lily Rose—'

She swallowed. 'Nik—'

'Don't be nervous.' He murmured the words against her lips. 'There's no reason to be nervous.'

'I'm not nervous,' she lied. 'But I'm not really sure what happens next.'

'I'll decide what happens next.'

Her heart bumped uncomfortably against her ribs. 'So—what do you want me to do?'

His mouth hovered close to hers and his fingers grazed her jaw. 'I want you to stop talking.'

'I'm going to stop talking right now this second.' Her stomach felt as if a thousand butterflies were trying to escape. She hadn't expected him to be so gentle, but those exploring fingers were slow, almost languorous as they stroked her face and slid over her neck and into her hair.

She stood, disorientated by intoxicating pleasure as he trailed his mouth along her jaw, tormenting her with dark, dangerous kisses. Heat uncurled low in her pelvis and spread through her body, sapping the strength from her knees, and she slid her hands over those sleek, powerful shoulders, feeling the hard swell of muscle beneath her palms. His mouth moved lower and she tilted her head back as he kissed her neck and then the base of her throat. She felt the slow slide of his tongue against supersensitive skin, the warmth of his breath and then his hand slid back into her hair and he brought his mouth back to hers. He kissed her with an erotic expertise that made her head spin and her legs grow heavy. With each slow stroke of his tongue, he sent her senses spinning out of control. It was like being drugged. She tried to find her balance, her centre, but just when she felt close to grasping a few threads of control, he used his mouth to drive every coherent thought from her head. Shaky, she lifted her hand to his face, felt the roughness of his jaw against her palm and the lean, spare perfection of his bone structure.

She slid her fingers into his hair and felt his hand slide down her spine and draw her firmly against him.

She felt him, brutally hard through the silky fabric of her dress, and she gave a moan, low in her throat as he trapped her there with the strength of his arms, the power in those muscles reminding her that this wasn't a safe flirtation, or a game.

His kisses grew rougher, more intimate, more demanding and she tugged at his shirt, her fingers swift and sure on the buttons, her movements more frantic with each bit of male muscle she exposed.

His chest was powerful, his abs lean and hard and she felt a moment of breathless unease because she'd never had sex with a man built like him.

He was self-assured and experienced and as she pushed the shirt from his shoulders she tried to take a step backwards.

'I'd like to keep my clothes on, if that's all right with you.'

'It's not all right.' But there was a smile in his voice as he slid his hand from her hips to her waist, pulling her back against him. His fingers brushed against the underside of her breast and she moaned.

'You look as if you spend every spare second of your life working out.'

'I don't.'

'You get this way through lots of athletic sex?'

His mouth hovered close to hers. 'You promised to stop talking.'

'That was before I saw you half naked. I'm intimidated. That photo didn't lie. Now I know what you look like under your clothes I think I might be having body-image problems.'

He smiled, and she felt his hands at the back of her dress and the slow slither of silk as her dress slid to the floor.

Standing in front of him in nothing but her underwear and high heels, she felt ridiculously exposed. It didn't matter that he'd already seen her that way. This was different.

He eased back from her, his eyes slumberous and dangerously dark. 'Let's go upstairs.'

Her knees were shaking so much she wasn't sure she could walk but the next moment he scooped her into his arms and she gave a gasp of shock and dug her hands in his shoulder.

'Don't you dare drop me. I bruise easily.' She had a close-up view of his face and stared hungrily at the hard masculine lines, the blue-black shadow of his jaw and the slim, sensual line of his mouth. 'If I'd known you were planning on carrying me I would have said no to dessert.'

'Dessert was the best part.' They reached the top of the stairs and he carried her into his bedroom and lowered her to the floor next to the bed.

She didn't see him move, and yet a light came on next to the bed sending a soft beam over the silk covers. Glancing around her, Lily realised that if she lay on that bed her body would be illuminated by the wash of light.

'Can we switch the lights off?'

His eyes hooded, he lowered his hands to his belt. 'No.' As he removed the last of his clothes she let her eyes skid downwards and felt heat pour into her cheeks.

It was only a brief glance, but it was enough to imprint the image of his body in her brain.

'Do you model underwear in your spare time? Because seriously—' Her cheeks flooded with colour. 'Okay so I think this whole thing would be easier in the dark—then I won't be so intimidated by your supersonic abs.'

'Hush.' He smoothed her hair back from her face. 'Do you trust me?' His voice was rough and she felt a flutter of nerves low in her belly.

'I—yes. I think so. Why? Am I being stupid?'

'No. Close your eyes.'

She hesitated and then closed them. She heard the sound of a drawer opening and then felt something soft and silky being tied round her eyes.

'What are you doing?' She lifted her hand but he closed his fingers round her wrist and drew her hands back to her sides.

'Relax.' His voice was a soft purr. 'I'm taking away one of your senses. The one that's making you nervous. There's no need to panic. You still have four remaining. I want you to use those.'

'I can't see.'

'Exactly. You wanted to do this in the dark. Now you're in the dark.'

'I meant that you should put the lights out! It was so you couldn't see me, not so that I couldn't see you.'

'Shh.' His lips nibbled at hers, his tongue stroking over her mouth in a slow, sensual seduction.

She was quivering, her senses straining with delicious anticipation as she tried to work out where he was and where he'd touch her next.

She felt his lips on her shoulder and felt his fingers slide the thin straps of her bra over her arms. Wetness pooled between her thighs and she pressed them together, so aroused she could hardly breathe.

He took his time, explored her neck, her shoulder, the underside of her breast until she wasn't sure her legs would hold her and he must have known that because he tipped her back onto the bed, supporting her as she lost her balance.

She could see nothing through the silk mask but she felt the weight of him on top of her, the roughness of his thigh against hers and the slide of silk against her heated flesh as he stripped her naked.

She was quivering, her senses sharpened by her lack of vision. She felt the warmth of his mouth close over the tip of her breast, the skilled flick of his tongue sending arrows of pleasure shooting through her over-sensitised body.

She gave a moan and clutched at his shoulders. 'Do we need a safe word or something?' She felt him pause.

'Why would you need a safe word?'

'I thought—'

'I'm not going to do anything that makes you uncomfortable.'

'What do I say if I want you to stop?'

His mouth brushed lightly across her jaw. 'You say "stop".'

'That's it?'

'That's it.' There was a smile in his voice. 'If I do one single thing that makes you uncomfortable, tell me.'

'Is embarrassed the same as uncomfortable?'

He gave a soft laugh and she felt the stroke of his palm on her thigh and then he parted her legs and his mouth drifted from her belly to her inner thigh.

He paused, his breath warm against that secret place. 'Relax, *erota mou*.'

She lifted her hands to remove the blindfold but he caught her wrists in one hand and held them pinned, while he used the other to part her and expose her secrets.

Unbearably aroused, melting with a confusing mix of desire and mortification, she tried to close her legs but he licked at her intimately, opening her with his tongue, exploring her vulnerable flesh with erotic skill and purpose until all she wanted was for him to finish what he'd started.

'Nik—' She writhed, sobbed, struggled against

him and he released her hands and anchored her hips, holding her trapped as he explored her with his tongue.

She'd forgotten all about removing the blindfold.

The only thing in her head was easing the maddening ache that was fast becoming unbearable.

She dug her fingers in the sheets, moaning as he slid his fingers deep inside her, manipulating her body and her senses until she tipped into excitement overload. She felt herself start to throb round those seeking fingers, but instead of giving her what she wanted he gently withdrew his hand and eased away from her.

'Please! Oh, please—' she sobbed in protest, wondering what he was doing.

Was he leaving her?

Was he stopping?

With a whimper of protest, she writhed and reached for him and then she heard a faint sound and understood the reason for the brief interlude.

Condom, she thought, and then the ability to think coherently vanished because he covered her with the hard heat of his body. She felt the blunt thrust of his erection at her moist entrance and tensed in anticipation, but instead of entering her he cupped her face in his hand and gently slid off the blindfold.

'Look at me.' His soft command penetrated her brain and she opened her eyes and stared at him dizzily just as he slid his hand under her bottom and entered her in a series of slow, deliciously skilful thrusts. He was incredibly gentle, taking his time, murmuring soft words in Greek and then English as he moved deep into the heart of her. Then he paused, kissed her mouth gently, holding her gaze with his.

'Are you all right? Do you want to use the safe word?' His voice was gently teasing but the glitter in his eyes and the tension in his jaw told her he was nowhere near as relaxed as he pretended to be.

In the grip of such intolerable excitement she was incapable of responding, Lily simply shook her head and then moaned as he withdrew slightly and surged into her again, every movement of his body escalating the wickedly agonising pleasure.

She slid her hands over the silken width of his shoulders, down his back, her fingers clamping over the thrusting power of his body as he rocked against her. His hand was splayed on her bottom, his gaze locked on hers as he drove into her with ruthlessly controlled strength and a raw, primitive rhythm. She wrapped her legs around him as he brought pleasure raining down on both of them.

She cried out his name and he took her mouth, kissing her deeply, intimately, as the first ripple of orgasm took hold of her body. They didn't stop kissing, mouths locked, eyes locked as her body contracted around his and dragged him over the edge of control. She'd never experienced anything like it, the whole experience a shattering revelation about her capacity for sensuality.

It was several minutes before she was capable of speaking and longer than that before she could persuade her body to move.

As she tried to roll away from him, his arms locked around her. 'Where do you think you're going?'

'I'm sticking to the rules. I thought this was a one-night thing.'

'It is.' He hauled her back against him. 'And the night isn't over yet.'

CHAPTER FIVE

NIK SPENT TEN minutes under a cold shower, trying to wake himself up after a night that had consisted of the worst sleep of his life and the best sex. He couldn't remember the last time he hadn't wanted to leave the bed in the morning.

A ton of work waited for him in the office, but for the first time ever he was contemplating working from home so that he could spend a few more hours with Lily. After her initial shyness she'd proved to be adventurous and insatiable, qualities that had kept both of them awake until the rising sun had sent the first flickers of light across the darkened bedroom.

Eventually she'd fallen into an exhausted sleep, her body tangled around his as dawn had bathed the bedroom in a golden glow.

It had proved impossible to extract himself without waking her so Nik, whose least favourite bedroom activity was hugging, had remained there, his senses bathed in the soft floral scent of her skin and hair, trapped by those long limbs wrapped trustingly around him.

And he had no one to blame but himself.

She'd offered to leave and he'd stopped her.

He frowned, surprised by his own actions. He had no need for displays of affection or any of the other meaningless rituals that seemed to inhabit other people's relationships. To him, sex was a physical need, no different from hunger and thirst. Once satisfied he moved on. He had no desire for anything deeper. He didn't believe anything deeper existed.

When he was younger, women had tried to persuade him differently. There had been a substantial number who had believed they had what it took to penetrate whatever steely coating made his heart so inaccessible. When they'd had no more success than their predecessors they'd withdrawn, bruised and broken, but not before they'd delivered their own personal diagnosis on his sorry condition.

He'd heard it all. That he didn't have a heart, that he was selfish, single minded, driven, too focused on his work. He accepted those accusations without argument, but knew that none explained his perpetually single status. Quite simply, he didn't believe in love. He'd learned at an early age that love could be withdrawn as easily as it was given, that promises could be made and broken in the same breath, that a wedding ring was no more than a piece of jewellery, and wedding vows no more binding than one plant twisted loosely around another.

He had no need for the friendship and affection that punctuated other people's lives.

He'd taught himself to live without it, so to find himself wrapped in the tight embrace of a woman who smiled even when she was asleep was as alien to him as it was unsettling.

For a while, he'd slept, too, and then woken to find her locked against him. Telling himself that she was the one holding him and not the other way round, he'd managed to extract himself without waking her and escaped to the bathroom where he contemplated his options.

He needed to find a tactful way of ejecting her.

He showered, shaved and returned to the bedroom. Expecting to find her still asleep, he was thrown to find her dressed. She'd stolen one of his white shirts and it fell to mid-thigh, the sleeves flapping over her small hands as she talked on the phone.

'Of course he'll be there.' Her voice was as soothing as warm honey. 'I'm sure it's a simple misunderstanding…well, no I agree with you, but he's very busy…'

She lay on her stomach on the bed, her hair hanging in a blonde curtain over one shoulder, the sheets tangled around her bare thighs.

Nik took one look at her and decided that there was no reason to rush her out of the villa.

They'd have breakfast on the terrace. Maybe enjoy a swim.

Then he'd find a position they hadn't yet tried before sending her home in his car.

Absorbed in her conversation, she hadn't noticed him and he strolled round in front of her and slowly released the towel from his waist.

He saw her eyes go wide. Then she gave him a smile that hovered somewhere between cheeky and innocent and he found himself resenting the person on the end of the phone who was taking up so much of her time.

He dressed, aware that she was watching him the whole time, her conversation reduced to soothing, sympathetic noises.

It was the sort of exchange he'd never had in his life. The sort that involved listening while someone poured out their woes. When Nik had a problem he solved it or accepted it and moved on. He'd never understood the female urge to dissect and confide.

'I know,' she murmured. 'There's nothing more upsetting than a rift in the family, but you need to talk. Clear the air. Be open about your feelings.'

She was so warm and sympathetic it was obvious to Nik that the conversation was going to be a long one. Someone had rung in the belief that talking to Lily would make them feel better and he couldn't see a way that this exchange would ever end as she poured a verbal Band-Aid over whatever wound she was being asked to heal. Who would want to hang up when they were getting the phone equivalent of a massive hug?

Outraged on her behalf, Nik sliced his finger across his throat to indicate that she should cut the connection.

When she didn't, he was contemplating snatching the phone and telling whoever it was to get a grip, sort out their own problems and stop encroaching on Lily's good nature when she gestured to the phone with her free hand.

'It's for you,' she mouthed. 'Your father.'

His *father*?

The person she'd been soothing and placating for the past twenty minutes was his *father*?

Nik froze. Only now did he notice that the phone in her hand was his. 'You answered my phone?'

'I wouldn't have done normally, but I saw it was your dad and I knew you'd want to talk to him. I didn't want you to miss his call because you were in the shower.' Clearly believing she'd done him an enormous favour, she wished his father a cheery, caring goodbye and held out the phone to him. The front of his shirt gapped, revealing those tempting dips and curves he'd explored in minute detail the night before. The scrape of his jaw had left faint red marks over her creamy skin and the fact that he instantly wanted to drop the phone in the nearest body of water and take her straight back to bed simply added to his irritation.

'That's my shirt.'

'You have so many, I didn't think you'd miss one.'

Reflecting on the fact she was as chirpy in the morning as she was the rest of the day, Nik dragged his gaze from her smiling mouth, took the phone from her and switched to Greek. 'You didn't need to call again. I got your last four messages.'

'Then why didn't you call me back?'

'I've been busy.'

'Too busy to talk to your own father? I have

rung you every day this week, Niklaus. Every single day.'

Aware that Lily was listening Nik paced to the window, turned his back on her and stared out over the sea. 'Is the wedding still on?'

'Of course it is on! Why wouldn't it be? I love Diandra and she loves me. You would love her, too, if you took the time to meet her and what better time than the day in which we exchange our vows?' There was a silence. 'Nik, come home. It has been too long.'

Nik knew exactly how long it had been to the day.

'I've been busy.'

'Too busy to visit your own family? This is the place of your birth and you never come home. You have a villa here that you converted and you don't even visit. I know you didn't like Callie and it's true that for a long time I was very angry with you for not making more of an effort when she showed you so much love, but that is behind us now.'

Reflecting on exactly what form that 'love' had taken, Nik tightened his hand on the phone and wondered if he'd been wrong not to tell his father the unpalatable truth about his third wife. He'd made the decision that since she'd ended the relationship anyway there was nothing to be gained from revealing the truth, but now he found himself in the rare position of questioning his own judgement.

'Will Callie be at the wedding?'

'No.' His father was quiet. 'I wanted her to bring little Chloe, but she hasn't responded to my calls. I don't mind admitting it's a very upsetting situation all round for everyone.'

Not everyone, Nik thought. He was sure Callie wasn't remotely upset. Why would she be? She'd extracted enough money from his father to ensure she could live comfortably without ever lifting a finger again. 'You would really want her at your wedding?'

'Callie, no. But Chloe? Yes, of course. If I had my way she would be living here with me. I still haven't given up hope that might happen one day. Chloe is my child, Nik. My daughter. I want her to grow up knowing her father. I don't want her thinking I abandoned her or chose not to have her in my life.'

Nik kept his eyes forward and the past firmly suppressed. 'These things happen. They're part of life and relationships.'

His father sighed. 'I'm sorry you believe that. Family is the most important thing in the world. I want that for you.'

'I set my own life goals, and that isn't on the list,' Nik drawled softly. Contemplating the complexity of human relationships, he was doubly glad he'd successfully avoided them himself. Like every other area of his life, he had his feelings firmly under control. 'Would Diandra really want Chloe to be living with you?'

'Of course! She'd be delighted. She wants it as much as I do. And she'd really like to meet you, too. She's keen for us to be a proper family.'

A proper family.

A long-buried memory emerged from deep inside his brain, squeezing itself through the many layers of self-protection he'd used to suppress it.

It had been so long the images were no longer clear, a fact for which he was grimly grateful. Even now, several decades later, he could still remember how it had felt to have those images replaying in his head night after night.

A man, a woman and a young boy, living an idyllic existence under blue skies and the dazzle of the sun. Growing up, he'd learned a thousand lessons about living. How to cook with leaves from the vine, how to distil the grape skins and seeds to form the potent *tsikoudia* they drank with friends. He'd lived his cocooned existence until one day his world had crumbled and he'd learned the most important lesson of all.

That a family was the least stable structure invented by man.

It could be destroyed in a moment.

'Come home, Niklaus,' his father said quietly. 'It has been too long. I want us to put the past behind us. Callie is no longer here.'

Nik didn't tell him that the reason he avoided the island had nothing to do with Callie.

Whenever he returned there it stirred up the same memory of his mother leaving in the middle of the night while he watched in confusion from the elegant curve of the stairs.

Where are you going, Mama? Are you taking us with you? Can we come, too?

'Niklaus?' His father was still talking. 'Will you come?'

Nik dragged his hand over the back of his neck. 'Yes, if that's what you want.'

'How can you doubt it?' There was joy in his father's voice. 'The wedding is Tuesday but many of our friends are arriving at the weekend so that we can celebrate in style. Come on Saturday then you can join in the pre-wedding celebrations.'

'Saturday?' His father expected him to stay for four days? 'I'll have to see if I can clear my diary.'

'Of course you can. What's the point of being in charge of the company if you can't decide your own schedule? Now tell me about Lily. I like her very much. How long have the two of you been together?'

Ten memorable hours. 'How do you know her name?'

'We've been talking, Niklaus! Which is more than you and I ever do. She sounds nice. Why don't you bring her to the wedding?'

'We don't have that sort of relationship.' He felt a flicker of irritation. Was that why she'd spent so much time on the phone talking to his father? Had she decided that sympathy might earn her an invite to the biggest wedding of the year in Greece?

Exchanging a final few words with his father, he hung up. 'Don't ever,' he said with silky emphasis as he turned to face her, 'answer my phone again.' But he was talking to an empty room because Lily was nowhere to be seen.

Taken aback, Nik glanced towards the bathroom and then noticed the note scrawled on a piece of paper by his pillow.

Thanks for the best rebound sex ever. Lily.

The best rebound sex?

She'd left?

Nik picked up the note and scrunched it in his palm. He'd been so absorbed in the conversation with his father he hadn't heard her leaving.

The dress from the night before lay neatly folded on the chair but there was no sign of the shoes or his shirt. He had no need to formulate a plan to eject her from his life because she'd removed herself.

She'd gone.

And she hadn't even bothered saying goodbye.

'No need to ask if you had a good night, it's written all over your face.' Brittany slid her feet into her hiking boots and reached for her bag. 'Nice shirt. Is that silk?' She reached out and touched the fabric and gave a murmur of appreciation. 'The man has style, I'll give him that.'

'Thanks for your text. It was sweet of you to check on me. How was your evening?'

'Nowhere near as exciting as yours apparently. While you were playing Cinderella in the wolf's lair, I was cataloguing pottery shards and bone fragments. My life is so exciting I can hardly bear it.'

'You love it. And I think you're mixing your

fairy tales.' Aware that her hair was a wild mass of curls after the relentless exploration of Nik's hands, Lily scooped it into a ponytail. She told herself that eventually she'd stop thinking about him. 'Did you find anything else after I left yesterday?'

'Fragments of plaster, conical cups—' Brittany frowned. 'We found a bronze leg that probably belongs to that figurine that was discovered last week. Are you listening to me?'

Lily was deep in an action replay of the moment Nik had removed the mask from her eyes. 'That's exciting! I'm going to join you later.'

'We're removing part of the stone mound and exploring the North Eastern wall.' Brittany eyed her. 'You might want to rethink white silk. So am I going to hear the details?'

'About what?'

'Oh, please—'

'It was fun. All right, incredible.' Lily felt her cheeks burn and Brittany gave a faint smile.

'That good? Now I'm jealous. I haven't had incredible sex since—well, let's just say it's been a while. So are you seeing him again?'

'Of course not. The definition of rebound sex is that it's just one night. No commitment.' She parroted the rules and tried not to wish it could have lasted a little more than one night. The truth was even in that one night Nik had made her feel special. 'Do we have food in our fridge? I'm starving.'

'He helped you expend all those calories and then didn't feed you before you left? That's not very gentlemanly.'

'He didn't see me leave. He had to take a call.' And judging from the reluctance he'd shown when she'd handed him the phone, if it had been left to him he wouldn't have answered it.

Why not?

Why wouldn't a man want to talk to his father?

It had been immediately obvious that whatever issues Nik might have in expressing his emotions openly weren't shared by his father, who had been almost embarrassingly eager to share his pain.

She'd squirmed with discomfort as Kostas Zervakis had told her how long it was since his son had come home. Even on such a short acquaintance she knew that family was one of the subjects Nik didn't touch. She'd felt awkward listening, as if she were eavesdropping on a private conversation, but at the same time his father had seemed so upset she hadn't had the heart to cut him off.

The conversation had left her feeling ever so slightly sick, an emotion she knew was ridiculous given that she hadn't ever met Kostas and barely knew his son. Why should it bother her that there were clearly problems in their relationship?

Her natural instinct had been to intervene but she'd recognised instantly the danger in that. Nik wasn't a man who appreciated the interference of others in anything, least of all his personal life.

The black look he'd given her had been as much responsible for her rapid exit as her own lack of familiarity with the morning-after etiquette following rebound sex.

She'd taken advantage of his temporary absorption in the phone call to make a hasty escape, but not before she'd heard enough to make her wish for a happy ending. Whatever damage lay in their past, she wanted them to fix their problems.

She always wanted people to fix their problems.

Lily blinked rapidly, realising that Brittany was talking. 'Sorry?'

'So he doesn't know you left?'

'He knows by now.'

'He won't be pleased that you didn't say goodbye.'

'He'll be delighted. He doesn't want emotional engagement. No awkward conversations. He will be relieved to be spared a potentially awkward conversation. We move in different circles so

I probably won't ever see him again.' And that shouldn't bother her, should it? Although a one-night stand was new to her, she was the expert at transitory relationships. Her entire life had been a series of transitory relationships. No one had ever stuck in her life. She felt like an abandoned railway station where trains passed through but never stopped.

Brittany glanced out of the window at the street below and raised her eyebrows. 'I think you're going to see him again a whole lot sooner than you think.'

'What makes you say that?'

'Because he's just pulled up outside our apartment.'

Lily's heart felt as if it were trying to escape from her chest. 'Are you sure?'

'Well there's a Ferrari parked outside that costs more than I'm going to earn in a lifetime, so, unless there is someone else living in this building that has attracted his attention, he clearly has things he wants to say to you.'

'Oh *no*.' Lily shrank against the door of the bedroom. 'Can you see his face? Does he look angry?'

'What reason would he have to be angry?' Brittany glanced out of the window again and then back at Lily. 'Is this about the shirt? He can afford to lose one shirt, surely?'

'I don't think he's here because of the shirt,' Lily said weakly. 'I think he's here because of something I did this morning. I'm going to hide on the balcony and you're going to tell him you haven't seen me.'

Brittany looked at her curiously. 'What did you do?'

Lily flinched as she heard a loud hammering on the door. 'Remember—you haven't seen me.' She fled into the bedroom they shared and closed the door.

What was he doing here?

She'd seen the flash of anger in his eyes when he'd realised it was *his* phone she'd answered, but surely he wouldn't care enough to follow her home?

She heard his voice in the doorway and heard Brittany say, 'Sure, come right on in, Nik—is it all right if I call you Nik?—she's in the bedroom, hiding.' The door opened a moment later and Brittany stood there, arms folded, her eyes alive with laughter.

Lily impaled her with a look of helpless fury. 'You're a traitor.'

'I'm a friend and I am doing you a favour,' Brittany murmured. 'The man is seriously *hot*.' Having delivered that assessment, she stepped to one side with a bright smile. 'Go ahead. The space is a little tight, but I guess you folks don't mind that.'

'No! Brittany, don't—er—hi...' Lily gave a weak smile as Nik strolled into the room. His powerful frame virtually filled the cramped space and she wished she'd picked a different room as a refuge. Being in a bedroom reminded her too much of the night before. 'If you're mad about the shirt, then give me two minutes to change. I shouldn't have taken it, but I didn't want to do the walk of shame through the middle of Chania wearing an evening dress that doesn't belong to me.'

'I don't care about the shirt.' His hair was glossy dark, his eyes dark in a face so handsome it would have made a Greek god weep with envy. 'Do you seriously think I'm here because of the shirt?'

'No. I assume you're mad because I answered your phone, but I saw that it was your father and thought you wouldn't want to miss his call. If I had a dad I'd be ringing him every day.'

His face revealed not a flicker of emotion. 'We don't have that sort of relationship.'

'Well I know that *now,* but I didn't know when I answered the phone and once he started talking he was so upset I didn't want to hang up. He needed to talk to someone and I was in the right place at the right time.'

'You think so?' His voice was silky soft. 'Because I would have said you were in the wrong place at the wrong time.'

'Depends how you look at it. Did you manage to clear the air?' She risked a glance at the hard lines of his face and winced. 'I'm guessing the answer to that is no. If I made it worse by handing you the phone, I'm sorry.'

He raised an eyebrow. 'Are you?'

She opened her mouth and closed it again. 'No, not really. Family is the most important thing in the world. I don't understand how anyone could not want to try and heal a rift. But I could see you were very angry that I'd answered the call and of course your relationship with your father is none of my business.' But she wanted to make it her business so badly she virtually had to sit on her hands to stop herself from interfering.

'For someone who realises it's none of her business, you seem to be showing an extraordinary depth of interest.'

'I feel strongly about protecting the family unit. It's my hot button.'

His searing glance reminded her he was intimately familiar with all her hot buttons. 'Why did you walk out this morning?'

The blatant reminder of the night before brought the colour rushing to her cheeks.

'I thought the first rule of rebound sex was that you rebound right out of the door the next morning. I have no experience of morning-after conversation and frankly the thought of facing you over breakfast after all the things we did last night didn't totally thrill me. And can you honestly tell me you weren't standing in that shower working out how you were going to eject me?' The expression on his face told her she was right and she nodded. 'Exactly. I thought I'd spare us both a major awkward moment and leave. I grabbed a shirt and was halfway out of the door when your father rang.'

'It didn't occur to you to ignore the phone?'

'I thought it might be important. And it was! He was *so* upset. He told me he'd already left a ton of messages.' Concern overwhelmed her efforts not to become involved. 'Why haven't you been home for the past few years?'

'A night in my bed doesn't qualify you to ask those questions.' The look in his eyes made her confidence falter.

'I get the message. Nothing personal. Now back

off. Last night you were charming and fun and flirty. This morning you're scary and intimidating.'

He inhaled deeply. 'I apologise,' he breathed. 'It was not my intention to come across as scary or intimidating, but you should *not* have answered the phone.'

'What's done is done. And I was glad to be a listening ear for someone in pain.'

'My father is not in pain.'

'Yes, he is. He misses you. This rift between you is causing him agony. He wants you to go to his wedding. It's breaking his heart that you won't go.'

'Lily—'

'You're going to tell me it's none of my business and you're right, it isn't, but I don't have a family at all. I don't even have the broken pieces of a family, and you have no idea how much I wish I did. So you'll have to forgive me if I have a tendency to try and glue back together everyone else's chipped fragments. It's the archaeologist in me.'

'Lily—'

'Just because you don't believe in love, doesn't mean you have to inflict that view on others and judge them for their decisions. Your father is happy and you're spoiling it. He loves you and he wants you there. Whatever you are feeling, you should bury it and go and celebrate. You should raise a glass and dance at his wedding. You should show him you love him no matter what, and if this marriage goes wrong then you'll be there to support him.' She stopped, breathless, and waited to be frozen by the icy wind of his disapproval but he surprised her yet again by nodding.

'I agree.'

'You do?'

'Yes. I've been trying to tell you that but you wouldn't stop talking.' He spoke through clenched teeth. 'I am convinced that I should go to the wedding, which is why I'm here.'

'What does the wedding have to do with me?'

'I want you to come with me.'

Lily gaped at him. 'Me? Why?'

He ran his hand over the back of his neck. 'I am willing to be present if that is truly what my father wants, but I don't have enough faith in my acting skills to believe I will be able to convince anyone that I'm pleased to be there. No matter how much he tells me Diandra is "the one", I cannot see how this match will have a happy ending. You, however, seem to see happy endings where none exist. I'm hoping that by taking you, people will be blinded in the dazzling beam of your sunny optimism and won't notice the dark thundercloud hovering close by threatening to rain on the proceedings.'

The analogy made her smile. 'You're the dark thundercloud in that scenario?'

His eyes gleamed. 'You need to ask?'

'You really believe this marriage is doomed? How can you say that when you haven't even met Diandra?'

'When it comes to women, my father has poor judgement. He follows his heart and his heart has no sense of direction. Frankly I can't believe he has chosen to get married again after three failed attempts. I think it's insane.'

'I think it's lovely.'

'Which is why you're coming as my guest.' He reached out and lifted a small blue plate from her shelf, tipping off the earrings that were stored there. 'This is stylish. Where did you buy it?'

'I didn't buy it, I made it. And I haven't agreed to come with you yet.'

'You *made* this?'

'It's a hobby of mine. There is a kiln at work and sometimes I use it. The father of one of the curators at the museum is a potter and he's helped me. It's interesting comparing old and new techniques.'

He turned it in his hands, examining it closely. 'You could sell this.'

'I don't want to sell it. I use it to store my earrings.'

'Have you ever considered having an exhibition?'

'Er—no.' She gave an astonished laugh. 'I've made about eight pieces I didn't throw away. They're all exhibited around the apartment. We use one as a soap dish.'

'You've never wanted to do this for a living?'

'What I want to do and what I can afford to do aren't the same thing. It isn't financially viable.' She didn't even allow her mind to go there. 'And where would our soap live? Let's talk about the wedding. A wedding is a big deal. It's intimate and special, an occasion to be shared with friends and loved ones. You don't even know me.' The moment the words left her mouth she realised how ridiculous that statement was given the night they'd spent. 'I mean obviously there are *some* things about me you know very well, but other things like my favourite flower and my favourite colour, you don't know.'

Still holding her plate, he studied her with an unsettling intensity. 'I know all I need to know, which is that you like weddings almost as much as I hate them. Did you study art?'

'Minoan art. This is a sideline. And if I go with you, people will speculate. How would you explain our relationship to your father? Would you want us to pretend to be in a relationship? Are we supposed to have known one another for ages or something?'

'No.' His frown suggested that option hadn't occurred to him. 'There is no need to tell anything other than the truth, which is that I'm inviting you to the wedding as a friend.'

'Friend with benefits?'

He put the plate back down on the shelf and replaced the earrings carefully. 'That part is strictly between us.'

'And if your father asks how we met?'

'Tell him the truth. He'd be amused, I assure you.'

'So you don't want to pretend we're madly in love or anything? I don't have to pose as your girlfriend?'

'No. You'd be going as yourself, Lily.' A muscle flickered in his lean jaw. 'God knows, the wedding will be stressful enough without us playing roles that feel unnatural.'

It was his obvious distaste for lies and games

that made up her mind. After David, a man whose instinct was to tell the truth was appealing. 'When would we leave?'

'Next Saturday. The wedding is on Tuesday but there will be four days of celebrations.' It was obvious from his expression he'd rather be dragged naked through an active volcano than join in those celebrations and a horrible thought crept into her mind.

'You're not going because you're planning to break off the wedding, are you?'

'No.' His gaze didn't shift from hers. 'But I won't tell you it didn't cross my mind.'

'I'm glad you rose above your natural impulse to wreck someone else's happiness. And if you really think it would help to have me there, then I'll come, if only to make sure you don't have second thoughts and decide to sabotage your father's big day.' Lily sank down onto the edge of her bed, thinking. 'I'll need to ask for time off.'

'Is that a problem? I could make a few calls.'

'No way!' Imagining how the curator at the museum would respond to personal intervention from Nik Zervakis, Lily recoiled in alarm. 'I'm quite capable of handling it myself. I don't need to bring in the heavy artillery, I'll simply ask the question. I'm owed holiday and my post ends in a couple of weeks anyway. Where exactly are we going? Where is "home" for you?'

'My father owns an island off the north coast of Crete. You will like it. The western part of the island has Minoan remains and there is a Venetian castle on one of the hilltops. It is separated from Crete by a lagoon and the beaches are some of the best anywhere in Greece. When you're not reminding me to smile, I'm sure you'll enjoy exploring.'

'And he *owns* this island? So tourists can't visit.'

'That's right. It belongs to my family.'

Lily looked at him doubtfully. 'How many guests will there be?'

'Does it matter?'

'I wondered, that's all.' She wanted to ask where they'd be sleeping but decided that if his father could afford a private island then presumably there wasn't a shortage of beds. 'I need to go shopping.'

'Given that you are doing me a favour, I insist you allow me to take care of that side of things.'

'No. Apart from last night, which wasn't real, I buy my own clothes. But thanks.'

'Last night didn't feel real?' He gave her a long, penetrating look and she felt heat rush into her cheeks as she remembered all the very real things he'd done to her and she'd done to him.

'I mean it wasn't really my life. More like a dreamy moment you know is never going to happen again.' Realising it was long past time she kept her mouth shut, she gave a weak smile. 'I'll buy or borrow clothes, don't worry. I'm good at putting together a wardrobe. Colours are my thing. The secret is to accessorise. I won't embarrass you even if we're surrounded by people dressed head to toe in Prada.'

'That possibility didn't enter my head. My concern was purely about the pressure on your budget.'

'I'm creative. It's not a problem.' She remembered she was wearing his shirt. 'I'll return this, obviously.'

A smile flickered at the corners of his mouth. 'It looks better on you than it does on me. Keep it.'

His gaze collided with hers and suddenly it was hard to breathe. Sexual tension simmered in the air and she was acutely aware of the oppressive heat in the small room that had no air conditioning. Blistering, blinding awareness clouded her vision until the only thing in her world was him. She wanted so badly to touch him. She wanted to lean into that muscled power, rip off those clothes and beg him to do all the things he'd done to her the night before. Shaken, she assumed she was alone in feeling that way and then saw something flare in his eyes and knew she wasn't. He was sexually aroused and thinking all the things she was thinking.

'Nik—'

'Saturday.' His tone was thickened, his eyes a dark, dangerous black. 'I will pick you up at eight a.m.'

She watched him leave, wondering what the rules of engagement were when one night wasn't enough.

CHAPTER SIX

NIK PUT HIS foot down and pushed the Ferrari to its limits on the empty road that led to the north-western tip of Crete.

He spent the majority of his time at the ZervaCo offices in San Francisco. When he returned to Crete it was to his villa on the beach near Chania, not to the island that had been his home growing up.

For reasons he tried not to think about, he'd avoided the place for the past few years and the closer he got to their destination, the blacker his mood.

Lily, by contrast, was visibly excited. She'd been waiting on the street when he'd arrived, her bag by her feet and she'd proceeded to question him non-stop. 'So will this be like *My Big Fat Greek Wedding*? I loved that movie. Will there be dancing? Brittany and I have been learning the *kalamatianós* at the *taverna* near our apartment so I should be able to join in as long as no one minds losing their toes.' She hummed a Greek tune to herself and he sent her an exasperated look.

'Are you ever *not* cheerful?'

The humming stopped and she glanced at him. 'You want me to be miserable? Did I misunderstand the brief, because I thought I was supposed to be the sunshine to your thundercloud. I didn't realise I had to be a thundercloud, too.'

Despite his mood, he found himself smiling. 'Are you capable of being a thundercloud?'

'I'm human. I have my low moments, same as anyone.'

'Tell me your last low moment.'

'No, because then I might cry and you'd dump me by the side of the road and leave me to be pecked to death by buzzards.' She gave him a cheery smile. 'This is the point where you reassure me that you wouldn't leave me by the side of the road, and that there are no buzzards in Crete.'

'There are buzzards. Crete has a varied habitat. We have vultures, Golden Eagle, kestrel—' he slowed down as he approached a narrow section of the road '—but I have no intention of leaving you by the side of the road.'

'I'd like to think that decision is driven by your inherent good nature and kindness towards your fellow man, but I'm pretty sure it's because you don't want to have to go to this wedding alone.'

'You're right. My actions are almost always driven by self-interest.'

'I don't understand you at all. I love weddings.'

'Even when you don't know the people involved?'

'I support the principle. I think it's lovely that your father is getting married again.'

Nik struggled to subdue a rush of emotion. 'It is not lovely that he is getting married again. It's ill advised.'

'That's your opinion. But it isn't what *you* think that matters, is it? It's what *he* thinks.' She spoke with gentle emphasis. 'And he thinks it's a good idea. For the record, I think it says a lot about a person that he is prepared to get married again.'

'It does.' As they hit a straight section of road, he pushed the car to its limits and the engine gave a throaty roar. 'It says he's a man with an inability to learn from his mistakes.'

'I don't see it that way.' Her hair whipped around her face and she anchored it with her hand and lifted her face to the sun. 'I think it shows optimism and I love that.'

Hearing the breathy, happy note in her voice he shook his head. 'Lily, how have you survived in this world without being eaten alive by unscrupulous people determined to take advantage of you?'

'I've been hurt on many occasions.'

'That doesn't surprise me.'

'It's part of life. I'm not going to let it shatter my belief in human nature. I'm an optimist. And what would it mean to give up? That would be like saying that love isn't out there, that it doesn't exist, and how depressing would *that* be?'

Nik, who lived his life firmly of the conviction that love didn't exist, didn't find it remotely depressing. To him, it was simply fact. 'Clearly you are the perfect wedding guest. You could set up a business, weddingguests.com. Optimists-R-us. You could be the guaranteed smile at every wedding.'

'Your cynicism is deeply depressing.'

'Your optimism is deeply concerning.'

'I prefer to think of it as inspiring. I don't want to be one of those people who think that a challenging past has to mean a challenging future.'

'You had a challenging past?' He remembered that she'd mentioned being brought up in foster care and hoped she wasn't about to give him the whole story.

She didn't. Instead she shrugged and kept her eyes straight ahead. 'It was a bit like a bad version of *Goldilocks and the Three Bears*. I was never "just right" for anyone, but that was my bad luck. I didn't meet the right family. Doesn't mean I don't believe there are loads of great families out there.'

'Doesn't what happened to you cause you to question the validity of any of these emotions you feel? The fact that the last guy lied to you *and* his wife doesn't put you off relationships?'

'It was one guy. I know enough about statistics to know you can't draw a reliable conclusion from a sample of one.' She frowned. 'If I'm honest, I'm working from a bigger sample than that because he's the third relationship I've had, but I still don't think you can make a judgement on the opposite sex based on the behaviour of a few.'

Nik, who had done exactly that, stayed silent and of course she noticed because she was nothing if not observant.

'Put it this way—if I'm bitten by a shark am I going to avoid swimming in the sea? I could, but then I'd be depriving myself of one of my favourite activities so instead I choose to carry on swimming and be a little more alert. Life isn't always about taking the safe option. Risk has to be balanced against the joy of living. I call it being receptive.'

'I call it being ridiculously naïve.'

She looked affronted. 'You're cross and irritable because you're not looking forward to this, but there is no reason to take it out on me. I'm here as a volunteer, remember?'

'You're right. I apologise.'

'Accepted. But for your father's sake you need to work on your body language. If you think you're a thundercloud you're deluding yourself because right now you're more of a tropical cyclone. You have to stop being judgemental and embrace what's happening.'

Nik took the sharp right-hand turn that led down to the beach and the private ferry. 'I am finding it hard to embrace something I know to be a mistake. It's like watching someone driving their car full speed towards a brick wall and not trying to do something to stop it.'

'You don't know it's a mistake,' she said calmly. 'And even if it is, he's an adult and should be allowed to make his own decisions. Now smile.'

He pulled in, killed the engine and turned to look at her.

Those unusual violet eyes reminded him of the spring flowers that grew high in the mountains. 'I will not be so hypocritical as to pretend I am pleased, but I promise not to spoil the moment.'

'If you don't smile then you *will* spoil the moment! Poor Diandra might take one look at your face and decide she doesn't want to marry into your family and then your father would be heart-broken. I can't believe I'm saying this, but be hyp-ocritical if that's what it takes to make you smile.'

'Poor Diandra will not be poor for long so I think it unlikely she'll let anything stand in the way of her wedding, even my intimidating pres-ence.'

Her eyes widened. 'Is that what this is about? You think she's after his money?'

'I have no idea but I'd be a fool not to consider it.' Nik saw no reason to be anything but honest. 'He is mega wealthy. She was his cook.'

'What does her occupation have to do with it? Love is about people, not professions. And I find it very offensive that you'd even think that. You can't judge a person based on their income. I know plenty of wealthy people who are slime-balls. In fact if we're going with stereotypes here, I'd say that generally speaking in order to amass great wealth you have to be prepared to be pretty ruthless. There are plenty of wealthy people who aren't that nice.'

Nik, who had never aspired to be 'nice', was careful not to let his expression change. 'Are you calling me a slimeball?'

'I'm simply pointing out that income isn't an indicator of a person's worth.'

'You mean because you don't know the level of expenditure?'

'No! Why is everything about money with you? I'm talking about *emotional* worth. Your father told me about Diandra. He was ill with flu last winter after Callie left. He was so ill at one point he couldn't drag himself from the bed. I sympathised because it happened to me once and I hope I never get flu again. Anyway, Diandra cared for him the whole time. She was the one who called the doctor. She made all his meals. That was kind, don't you think?'

'Or opportunistic.'

'If you carry on thinking like that you are going to die lonely. He met her when she cooked him her special moussaka to try and tempt him to eat. I *love* that he doesn't care what she does.'

'He should care. She stands to gain an enormous amount financially from this wedding.'

'That's horrible.'

'It is truly horrible. Finally we find something we agree on.'

'I wasn't agreeing with you! It's your attitude that's horrible, not this wedding. You're not only a judgemental cynic, you're also a raging snob.'

Nik breathed deeply. 'I am not a raging snob, but I am realistic.'

'No, what you are is damaged. Not everything has a price, Nik, and there are things in life that are far more important than money. Your father is trying to make a family and I think that's admirable.' She fumbled with the seat belt. 'Get me out of this car before I'm contaminated by you. Your thundercloud is about to rain all over my sunny patch of life.'

Your father is trying to make a family.

Nik thought about everything that had gone before.

He'd buried the pain and hurt deep and it was something he had never talked about with anyone, especially not his father, who had his own pain to deal with. What would happen when this relationship collapsed?

'If my father entered relationships with some degree of caution and objective contemplation then I would be less concerned, but he makes the same mistake you make. He confuses physical intimacy with love.' He saw the colour streak across her cheeks.

'I'm not confused. Have I spun fairy tales about the night we spent together? Have I fallen in love with you? No. I know exactly what it was and what we did. You're in a little compartment in my brain labelled "Once in a Lifetime Experiences" along with skydiving and a helicopter flight over the New York skyline. It was amazing by the way.'

'The helicopter flight was amazing?'

'No, I haven't done that yet. I was talking about the night with you, although there were moments that felt as nerve-racking as skydiving.' Her mouth tilted into a self-conscious smile. 'Of course it's also a little embarrassing looking at you in daylight after all those things we did in the dark, but I'm trying not to think about it. Now stop being annoying. In fact, stop talking for a while. That way I'm less likely to kill you before we arrive.'

Nik refrained from pointing out she'd been the only one in the dark. He'd had perfect vision and he'd used it to his own shameless advantage. There wasn't a single corner of her body he hadn't explored and the memory of every delicious curve was welded in his brain.

He tried to work out what it was about her that was so appealing. Innocence wasn't a quality he generally admired in a person so he had to assume the power of the attraction stemmed from the sheer novelty of being with someone who had managed to retain such an untarnished view of the world.

'Are you embarrassed about the night we spent together?'

'I would be if I thought about it, so I'm not thinking about it. I'm living in the moment.' Having offered that simple solution to the problem, she reached into the back of the car for her hat. 'You could take the same approach to the wedding. You're not here to fix it or protect anyone. You're here as a guest and your only responsibility is to smile and look happy. Is this it? Are we here? Because I don't see an island. Maybe your father might have changed the venue when he saw the black cloud of your presence approaching over the horizon.'

Nik dragged his gaze from her mouth to the jetty. 'This is it. From here, we go by boat.'

Lily stood in the prow of the boat feeling the cool brush of the wind on her face and tasting the salty air. The boat skimmed and bounced over the sparkling ocean towards the large island in the distance, sending a light spray over her face and tangling her hair.

Nik stood behind the wheel, legs braced, eyes hidden behind a pair of dark glasses. Despite the unsmiling set of his mouth, he looked more approachable and less the hard-headed businessman.

'This is so much fun. I think I might love it more than your Ferrari.'

He gave a smile that turned him from insanely good-looking to devastating, and she felt the intensity of the attraction like a physical punch.

It was true he didn't seem to display any of the family values that were so important to her, but that didn't do anything to diminish the sexual attraction.

As far as she could tell, he couldn't be more perfect for a short-term relationship.

For the whole trip in the car she'd been aware of him. As he'd shifted gear his hand had brushed against her bare thigh and she'd discovered that being with him was an exciting, exhilarating experience that was like nothing she'd experienced before.

There had been a brief moment when they'd pulled into the car park that she'd thought he might be about to kiss her. He'd looked at her mouth the way a panther looked at its prey before it devoured it, but just when she'd been about to close her eyes and take a fast ride to bliss, he'd sprung from the car, leaving her to wonder if she'd imagined it.

She'd followed him to the jetty, watching in fascination as the group of people gathered there sprang to attention. If she needed any more evidence of the power he wielded, she had only to observe the way people responded to him. He behaved with an authority that was instinctive, his air of command unmistakable even in this apparently casual setting.

It was a good job he didn't possess any of the qualities she was looking for, she thought, otherwise she'd be in trouble.

Her gaze lingered on his bronzed throat, visible at the open neck of his shirt. He handled the boat with the same confident assurance he displayed in everything and she was sure that no electrical device had ever dared to misbehave under his expert touch.

Trying not to think about just how expert his touch had been, she anchored her hair and shouted above the wind. 'The beaches are beautiful. People aren't allowed to bathe here?'

'You can bathe here. You're my guest.' As they approached the island, he slowed the speed of the boat and skilfully steered against the dock.

Two men instantly jumped forward to help and Nik sprang from the boat and held out his hand to her.

'I need to get my bag.'

'They will bring our luggage up to the villa later.'

'I have a gift for your father and it's only one bag,' she muttered. 'I can carry a single bag.'

'You bought a gift?'

'Of course. It's a wedding. I couldn't come without a small gift.' She stepped out of the bobbing boat and allowed herself to hold his hand for a few seconds longer than was necessary for balance. She felt warmth and strength flow through her fingers and had to battle the temptation to press herself against him. 'So how many bedrooms does your father have? Are you sure there is room for me to stay?'

The question seemed to amuse him. 'There will be room, *theé mou*, don't worry. As well as the main villa, there are several other properties scattered around the island. We will be staying in one of those.'

As they walked up a sandy path she breathed in the wonderful scents of sea juniper and wild thyme. 'One of the things I love most about Crete is the thyme honey. Brittany and I eat it for breakfast.'

'My father keeps bees so he will be very happy to hear you say that.'

The path forked at the top and he turned right

and took the path that led down to another beach. There, nestling in the small horseshoe bay of golden sand with the water almost lapping at the whitewashed walls, was a beautiful contemporary villa.

Lily stopped. '*That's* your father's house?' The position was idyllic, the villa stunning, but it looked more like a honeymoon hideaway than somewhere to accommodate a large number of high-profile international guests.

'No. This is Camomile Villa. The main house is fifteen minutes' walk in the other direction, towards the small Venetian fort. I thought we'd unpack and breathe for an hour or so before we face the guests.'

Witnessing his tension, she felt a rush of compassion. 'Nik—' She put her hand on his cheek and turned his face to hers. 'This is a wedding, not the sacking of Troy. You do not need to find your strength or breathe. Your role is to smile and enjoy yourself.'

His gaze locked on hers and she wished she hadn't touched him. His blue-shadowed jaw was rough beneath her fingers and suddenly she was remembering that night in minute detail.

Seriously unsettled, she started to pull her hand

away but he caught her wrist in his fingers and held it there.

'You are a very unusual woman.' His voice was husky and she gave a faint smile, ignoring the wild flutter of nerves low in her stomach.

'I am not even going to ask what you mean by that. I'm simply going to take it as a compliment.'

'Of course you are.' There was a strange gleam in his eyes. 'You see positive in everything, don't you?'

'Not always.' She could have told him that she saw very little positive in being alone in the world, having no family, but given his obvious state of tension she decided to keep that confidence to herself. 'So how do you know we're staying in Camomile Villa? Cute name, by the way. Maybe your father has given it to one of the other guests. Shouldn't you go and check?'

'Camomile belongs to me.'

Lily digested that. 'So actually you own five properties, not four.'

'I don't count this place.'

'Really? Because if I owned this I'd be spending every spare minute here.' She walked up the path, past silvery green olive trees, nets lying on the ground ready for harvesting later in the year. A small lizard lay basking in the hot sun and she smiled as it sensed company and darted for safety into the dry, dusty earth.

The path leading down to the villa cut through a garden of tumbling colour. Bougainvillaea in bright pinks and purples blended and merged against the dazzling white of the walls and the perfect blue of the sky.

Nik opened the door and Lily followed him inside.

White beamed ceilings and natural stone floors gave the interior a cool, uncluttered feel and the elegant white interior was lifted by splashes of Mediterranean blue.

'If you don't want this place, I might live here.' Lily looked at the shaded terrace with its beautiful infinity pool. 'Why does anyone need a pool when the sea is five steps from the front door?'

'Some people don't like swimming in the sea.'

'I'm not one of those people. I adore the sea. Nik, this place is—' she felt a lump in her throat '—it's really special.'

He opened the doors to the terrace and gave her a wary look. 'Are you going to cry?'

'It's perfect.' She blinked. 'And I'm fine. Happy. And excited. I love Crete, but I never get the chance to enjoy it like a tourist. I'm always working.' And never in her life had she experienced this level of luxury.

She and Brittany were always moaning about the mosquitoes and lack of air conditioning in their tiny apartment. At night they slept with the windows open to make the most of the breeze from the sea, but in the summer months it was almost unbearable indoors.

'You are the most unusual woman I've ever met. You enjoy small things.'

'This is not a small thing. And you're the unusual one.' She picked up her bag. 'You take this life for granted.'

'That is not true. I know how fortunate I am.'

'I don't think you do, but I'm going to be pointing it out to you every minute for the next few days so hopefully by the time we leave you will.' She glanced around her and then looked at him expectantly. 'My bedroom?'

For a wild, unnerving moment she hoped he was going to tell her there was just one bedroom, but he gestured to a door that led from the large spacious living area.

'The guest suite is through there. Make yourself comfortable.'

Guest suite.

So he didn't intend them to share a room. For Nik, it really had been one night.

Telling herself it was probably for the best, she followed his directions and walked through an open door into a bright, airy bedroom. The bed was draped in layers of cream and white, deep piles of cushions and pillows inviting the occupant to lounge and relax. The walls were hung with bold, contemporary art, slashes of deep blue on large canvases that added a stylish touch to the room. In one corner stood a tall, elegant vase in graduated blues, the colour shifting under the dazzling sunlight.

Lily recognised it instantly. 'That's one of Skylar's pots.'

He looked at her curiously. 'You know the artist?'

'Skylar Tempest. She and Brittany were roommates at college. They're best friends, as close as sisters. I would know her work anywhere. Her style, her use of colour and composition is unique, but I know that pot specifically because I talked to her about it. Brittany introduced us because Skylar wanted to talk to me about ceramics. She's incorporated a few Minoan designs into some of her work, modernised, of course.' She knelt down and slid her hand over the smooth surface of the glass. 'This is from her *Mediterranean Sky* collection. She had a small exhibition in New York, not only glass and pots but jewellery and a couple of paintings. She's insanely talented.'

'You were at that exhibition?'

'Sadly no. I don't move in those circles. Nor do I pretend to claim any credit for any of her incredible creations, but I did talk to her about shapes and style. Of course the Minoans used terracotta clay. It was Sky's idea to reproduce the shape in glass. Look at this—' She trailed her finger lightly over the surface. 'The Minoans usually decorated their pots with dark on light motifs, often of sea creatures, and she's taken her inspiration from that. It's genius. I can't believe you own it. Where did you find it?'

'I was at the exhibition.'

'In New York? How did you even know about her?'

'I saw her work in a small artisan jewellers in Greenwich Village and I bought one of her necklaces for—' He broke off and Lily looked at him expectantly.

'For? For one of your women? We're not in a relationship, Nik. You don't have to censor your conversation. And even if we were in a relationship you still wouldn't need to censor it.'

'In my experience, most women do not appreciate hearing about their predecessors.'

'Yes, well the more I hear about the women you've known in your life, the more I'm not surprised. Now tell me about how you discovered Skylar.'

'I asked to see more of her work and was told she was having an exhibition. I managed to get myself invited.'

Lily rocked back on her heels. 'She never mentioned that she met you.'

'We never met. I didn't introduce myself. I went on the first night and she was surrounded by well-wishers, so I simply bought a few pieces and left. That was two years ago.'

'So she doesn't know she sold pieces to Nik Zervakis?'

'A member of my team handled the actual transaction.'

Lily scrambled to her feet. 'Because you don't touch real money? She would be so excited if she knew her work was here in your villa. Can I tell her?'

He looked amused. 'If you think it would interest her, then yes.'

'Interest her? Of course it would interest her.' Lily pulled her phone out of her bag and took a photo. 'I must admit that pot looks perfect there. It needs a large room with lots of light. Did you know she has another exhibition coming up?' She slipped her phone back into her bag. 'December in London. An upmarket gallery in Knightsbridge is showing her work. She's really excited. Her new collection is called *Ocean Blue*. It's still sea themed. Brittany showed me some photos.'

'Will you be going?'

'To an exhibition in Knightsbridge? Sure. I thought I'd fly in on my private jet, spend a night in the Royal Suite at The Savoy and then get my driver to take me to the exhibition.' She laughed and then saw something flicker in his eyes. 'Er— that's exactly what you're going to be doing, isn't it?'

'My plans aren't confirmed.'

'But you do have a private jet.'

'ZervaCo owns a Gulfstream and a couple of Lear jets.' He said it as if it was normal and she shook her head, trying not to be intimidated.

For her, wealth was people and family, not money, but still—

'Seriously, Nik. What am I doing here? To you a Gulfstream is a mode of transport, to me it's a warm Atlantic current. I used to own a rusty mountain bike until the wheel fell off. I'm the one who works in a dusty museum, digs in the dirt in the summer and cleans other people's houses to give myself enough money to live. And living doesn't include jetting across Europe to a friend's exhibition. I have no idea where I'll even be in December. I'm job hunting.'

'Wherever you are, I'll fly you there. And for your information, I wouldn't be staying in the Royal Suite.'

'Because you already own an apartment that most royals would kill for.' His lack of response told her she was right and she rolled her eyes. 'Nik, we had an illuminating conversation earlier during which you confessed that you think your new stepmother is only interested in your father's money. Money is obviously a very big deal to you, so I'm hardly likely to take you up on your offer of a ride in your private jet, am I?'

'That is different. I'm grateful that you agreed to come here with me,' he said softly, 'and taking you to Skylar's exhibition would be my way of saying thank you.'

'I don't need a thank you. And to be honest I'm here because of the conversation I had with your father. My decision didn't have anything to do with you. We had one night, that's all. I mean, the sex was great, but I had no trouble walking out of your door that morning. There were no feelings involved.' She shook her head to add emphasis. 'Kevlar, that's me.'

He gave her a long, steady look. 'I have never met anyone who less resembles that substance.'

'Up until a week ago I would have agreed with you, but now I'm a changed person. Seriously, I'm enjoying being with you. You're smoking hot and surprisingly entertaining despite your warped view of relationships, but I am no more in love with you than I am with your supersonic shower. And you don't owe me anything for bringing me here—in fact I owe you.' She glanced across the room to the terrace outside. 'This is the nearest I've come to a vacation in a long time. It's not exactly a hardship being here. I am going to lie in the sun like that lizard out there.'

'You haven't met my family yet.' He paused, his gaze fixed on hers. 'Think about it. If you change your mind about coming to Skylar's London exhibition, let me know. The invitation stands. I won't withdraw it.'

It was a different world.

What would it be like, she wondered, not to have to think about your budget? Not to have to make choices between forfeiting one thing to buy another?

This close she could see the flecks of gold in those dark eyes, the blue-black shadow of his jaw and the almost unbelievably perfect lines of his bone structure. If a scale had been invented to measure sex appeal, she was pretty sure he would have shattered it. She couldn't look at his mouth without remembering all the ways he'd used it on her body and remembering made her want it again. She wanted to reach out and slide her fingers into that silky dark hair and press her mouth to his. And this time she wanted to do it without the blindfold.

Aware that her mind was straying into forbidden territory she took a step back, reminding herself that money came a poor second to family and this man seemed to be virtually estranged from his father.

'I won't change my mind.'

Dragging her gaze from his, she dropped her bag on the floor and unzipped it. 'I need to hang up my dresses or they'll be creased. I don't want to make a bad impression.'

'There are staff over in the main villa who will help you unpack. I can call them.'

'Are you kidding?' Amused by yet more evidence of the differences between their respective lifestyles, she pulled out her clothes. 'This will take me five minutes at most. And I'd be embarrassed to ask anyone else to hang up a tee shirt that cost the same amount as a cup of coffee. So what happens next?'

'We are joining my father and Diandra for lunch.'

'Sounds good to me.'

The expression on his face told her he didn't share her sentiments. 'I need to make some calls. Make yourself at home. The fridge is stocked, there are books in the living room. Feel free to use the pool. If there is anything you need, let me know. I'll be using the office on the other side of the living room.'

What else could she possibly need?

Lily glanced round the villa, which was by far the most luxurious and exclusive place she'd ever stayed.

She had a feeling the only thing she was going to need was a reality check.

He hadn't been back here since that summer five years before. It had been an attempt to put the past behind him, but ironically it had succeeded only in making things worse.

The memory of his last visit sat in his head like a muddy stain.

Nik strolled out onto the terrace, hoping the view would relieve his tension, but being here took him right back to his childhood and that was a place he made a point of avoiding.

With a soft curse, he walked back into the room he'd had converted into an office and switched on his laptop.

For the next hour he took an endless stream of calls and then finally, when he couldn't postpone the moment any longer, he took a quick shower and changed for lunch.

Another day, another wedding.

Mouth grim, he pocketed his phone and strolled through the villa to find Lily.

She was sitting in the shade on the terrace, a glass of iced lemonade by her hand and a book in her lap, staring out across the bright turquoise blue of the bay.

She hadn't noticed him and he stood for a moment, watching her. The tension left him to be replaced by tension of a different source. That one night he'd spent with her hadn't been anywhere near long enough.

He wanted to rip off that pretty blue sundress and take her straight back to bed but he knew that, no matter what she said, she wasn't the sort of woman to be able to keep her emotions out of the bedroom so he gave her a cool smile as he strolled onto the terrace.

'Are you ready?'

'Yes.' She slid her feet into a pair of silver ballet flats and put her book on the table. 'Is there anything I should know? Who will be there?'

'My father and Diandra. They wanted this lunch to be family only.'

'In other words your father doesn't want your first meeting for a long while to be in public.' She reached for her glass and finished her drink. 'Don't worry about me while we're here. I'm sure I can find a few friendly faces to talk to while you're mingling.'

He looked down at the curve of her cheeks and the dimple in the corner of her mouth and decided she was the one with the friendly face. If he had to pick a single word to describe her, it would be approachable. She was warm, friendly and he was sure there would be no shortage of guests eager to talk to her. The thought should have reduced his stress because it gave him one less responsibility, but it didn't.

Despite her claims to being made of Kevlar, he wasn't convinced she'd managed to manufacture even a thin layer of protection for herself.

He offered to drive her to avoid the heat but

she chose to walk and on the way up to the main house she grilled him about his background. Did his father still work? What exactly was his business? Did he have any other family apart from Nik?

His suspicion that she was more comfortable with this gathering than him was confirmed as soon as he walked onto the terrace.

He saw the table by the pool laid for four and felt Lily sneak her hand into his.

'He wants you to get to know Diandra. He's trying to build bridges,' she said softly, her fingers squeezing his. 'Don't glare.'

Before he could respond, his father walked out onto the terrace.

'Niklaus—' His voice shook and Nik saw the shimmer of tears in his father's eyes.

Lily extracted her hand from his. 'Hug him.' She made it sound simple and Nik wondered whether bringing someone as idealistic as Lily to a reunion as complicated as this one had been entirely sensible, but she and his father obviously thought alike because he walked towards them, arms outstretched.

'It's been too long since you were home. Far too long, but the past is behind us. All is forgiven. I have such news to tell you, Niklaus.'

Forgiven?

His feet nailed to the floor by the past and the weight of the secrets his father didn't know, Nik didn't move and then he felt Lily's small hand in his back pushing, harder this time, and he then stepped forward and was embraced by his father so tightly it knocked the air from his lungs.

He felt a heaviness in his chest that had nothing to do with the intensity of his father's grip. Emotions rushed towards him and he was beginning to wish he'd never agreed to this reunion when Lily stepped forward, breaking the tension of the moment with her warmest, brightest smile and an extended hand that gave his father no choice but to release Nik.

'I'm Lily Rose. We spoke on the phone. You have a very beautiful home, Mr Zervakis. It's kind of you to invite me to share your special day.' Blushing charmingly, she then attempted to speak a few words of Greek, a gesture that both distracted his father and guaranteed a lifetime of devotion.

Nik watched as his dazzled father melted like butter left in the hot sun.

He kissed her hand and switched to heavily accented English. 'You are welcome in my home, Lily. I'm so happy you are able to join us for what is turning out to be the most special week of my life. This is Diandra.'

For the first time Nik noticed the woman hovering in the background.

He'd assumed she was one of his father's staff, but now she stepped forward and quietly introduced herself.

Nik noticed that she didn't quite meet his eye, instead she focused all her attention on Lily as if she were the lifebelt floating on the surface of a deep pool of water.

Diandra clearly had sophisticated radar for detecting sympathy in people, Nik thought, wondering what 'news' his father had for them.

Experience led him to assume it was unlikely to be good.

'I've brought you a small gift. I made it myself.' Lily delved into her bag and handed over a prettily wrapped parcel.

It was a ceramic plate, similar to the one he'd admired in her apartment, decorated with the same pattern of swirling blues and greens.

Nik could see she had real talent and so, apparently, did his father.

'You made this? But this isn't your business?'

'No. I'm an archaeologist. But I did my dissertation on Minoan ceramics so it's an interest of mine.'

'You must tell me all about it. And all about yourself. Lily Rose is a beautiful name.' His father led her towards the table that had been laid next to the pool. Silver gleamed in the sunlight and bowls of olives gleamed glossy dark in beautiful blue bowls. Kostas put Lily's plate in the centre of the table. 'Your mother liked flowers?'

'I don't know. I didn't know my mother.' She shot Nik an apologetic look. 'That's too much information for a first meeting. Let's talk about something else.'

But Kostas Zervakis wasn't so easily deflected. 'You didn't know your mother? She passed away when you were young, *koukla mou*?'

Appalled by that demonstration of insensitivity, Nik shot him an exasperated look and was about to steer the conversation away from such a deeply personal topic when Lily answered.

'I don't know what happened to her. She left me in a basket in Kew Gardens in London when I was a few hours old.'

Whatever he'd expected to hear, it hadn't been that and Nik, who made a point of never asking about a woman's past, found himself wanting to know more. 'A basket?' Her eyes lifted to his and for a moment the presence of other people was forgotten.

'Yes. I was found by one of the staff and taken to hospital. They called me Lily Rose because I was found among the flowers. They never traced my mother. They assumed she was a teenager who panicked.' She spoke in a matter-of-fact tone but Nik knew she wasn't matter-of-fact about the way she felt.

This was why she had shown so much wistful interest in the detail of his family. At the time he hadn't been able to understand why it would make an interesting topic of conversation, but now he understood that, to her, it was not a frustration or a complication. It was an aspiration.

This was why she dreamed of happy endings, both for herself and other people.

He felt something stir inside him, an emotion that was entirely new to him.

He'd believed himself immune to even the most elaborately constructed sob story, but Lily's revelation had somehow managed to slide under those steely layers of protection he'd constructed for himself. For some reason, her simply stated story touched him deeply.

Unsettled, he dragged his eyes from her soft mouth and promised himself that no matter how much he wanted her, he wasn't going to touch her again. It wouldn't be fair, when their expectations of life were so different. He had no concerns about his own ability to keep a relationship superficial. He did, however, have deep concerns about her ability to do the same and he didn't want to hurt her.

His father, predictably, was visibly moved by the revelation about her childhood.

'No family?' His voice was roughened by emotion. 'So who raised you, *koukla mou*?'

'I was brought up in a series of foster homes.' She poked absently at her food. 'And now I think we should talk about something else because this is *definitely* too much detail for a first meeting, especially when we're here to celebrate a wedding.' Superficially she was as cheerful as ever but Nik knew she was upset.

He was about to make another attempt to change the topic when his father reached out and took Lily's hand.

'One day you will have a family of your own. A big family.'

Nik ground his teeth. 'I don't think Lily wants to talk about that right now.'

'I don't mind.' Lily sent him a quick smile and then turned back to his father. 'I hope so. I think family makes you feel anchored and I've never had that.'

'Anchors keep a boat secured in one place,' Nik said softly, 'which can be limiting.'

Her gaze met his and he knew she was deciding if his observation was random or a warning.

He wasn't sure himself. All he knew was that he didn't want her thinking this was anything other then temporary. He could see she'd had a tough life. He didn't want to be the one to shatter that optimism and remove the smile from her face.

His father gave a disapproving frown. 'Ignore him. When it comes to relationships my son behaves like a child in a sweetshop. He gorges his appetites without learning the benefits of selectivity. He enjoys success in everything he touches except, sadly, his private life.'

'I'm very selective.' Nik reached for his wine. 'And given that my private life is exactly the way I want it to be, I consider it an unqualified success.'

He banked down the frustration, wondering how his father, thrice divorced, could consider himself an example to follow.

His father looked at him steadily. 'All the money in the world will not bring a man the same feeling of contentment as a wife and children, don't you agree, Lily?'

'As someone with massive college loans, I wouldn't dismiss the importance of money,' Lily said honestly, 'but I agree that family is the most important thing.'

Feeling as if he'd woken up on the set of a Hollywood rom-com in which he'd been cast in the role of 'bad guy', Nik refrained from asking his father which of his wives had ever given him anything other than stomach ulcers and astronomical bills. Surely even he couldn't reframe his romantic past as anything other than a disaster.

'One day you will have a family, Lily.' Kostas Zervakis surveyed her with misty eyes and Nik observed this emotional interchange with something between disbelief and despair.

His father had known Lily for less than five minutes and already he was ready to leave her everything in his will. It was no wonder he'd made himself a target for every woman with a sob story.

Callie had spotted that vulnerability and dug her claws deep. No doubt Diandra was working on the same soft spot.

A dark, deeply buried memory stirred in the depths of his brain. His father, sitting alone in the bedroom among the wreckage of his wife's hasty packing, the image of wretched despair as she drove away without looking back.

Never, before or since, had Nik felt as power-less as he had that day. Even though he'd been a young child, he'd known he was witnessing pain beyond words.

The second time it had happened, he'd been a teenager and he remembered wondering why his father would have risked putting himself through such emotional agony a second time.

And then there had been Callie...

He'd known from the first moment that the re-lationship was doomed and had blamed himself later for not trying to save his father from that particular mistake.

And now here he was again, trapped in the unenviable position of having to make a choice between watching his father walk into another re-lationship disaster, or potentially damaging their relationship by trying to intervene.

Lily was right that his father was a grown man, able to make his own decisions. So why did he still have this urge to push his father out of the path of the oncoming train?

Emotions boiling inside him, he glanced across the table to his future stepmother, wondering if it was a coincidence that she'd picked the chair as far from his as possible.

She was either shy or she was harbouring a guilty conscience.

He'd promised he wouldn't interfere, but he was fast rethinking that decision.

He sat in silence, observing rather than participating, while staff discreetly served food and topped up glasses.

His father engaged Lily in conversation, encouraging her to talk about her life and her love of archaeology and Greece.

Forced to sit through a detailed chronology of Lily's life history, Nik learned that she'd had three boyfriends, worked numerous low-paid jobs to pay for college tuition, was allergic to cats, suffered from severe eczema as a child and had never lived in the same place for more than twelve months.

The more he discovered about her life, the more he realised how hard it had been. She'd made a joke about Cinderella, but Lily made Cinderella look like a slacker.

Learning far more than he'd ever wanted to know, he turned to his father. 'What is the "news" you have for me?'

'You will find out soon enough. First, I am enjoying having the company of my son. It's been too long. I have resorted to the Internet to find news of what is happening with you. You have been spending a great deal of time in San Francisco.'

Happy to talk about anything that shifted the focus from Lily, Nik relaxed slightly and talked broadly about some of the technology developments his company was spearheading and touched lightly on the deal he was about to close, but the diversion proved to be brief.

Kostas spooned olives onto Lily's plate. 'You must persuade Nik to take you to the far side of the island to see the Minoan remains. You will need to go early in the day, before it is too hot. At this time of year everything is very dry. If you love flowers, then you will love Crete in the spring. In April and May the island is covered in poppies, daisies, camomile, iris.' He beamed at her. 'You must come back here then and visit.'

'I'd like that.' Lily tucked into her food. 'These olives are delicious.'

'They come from our own olive groves and the lemonade in your fridge came from lemons grown on our own trees. Diandra made it. She is a genius in the kitchen. You wait until you taste her lamb.' Kostas leaned across and took Diandra's hand. 'I took one mouthful and fell in love.'

Losing his appetite, Nik gave her a direct look.

'Tell me about yourself, Diandra. Where were you brought up?' He caught Lily's urgent glance and ignored it, instead listening to Diandra's stammered response.

From that he learned that she was one of six children and had never been married.

'She never met the right person, and that is lucky for me,' his father said indulgently.

Nik opened his mouth to speak, but Lily got there first.

'You're so lucky having been born in Greece,' she said quickly. 'I've travelled extensively in the islands but living here must be wonderful. I've spent three summers on Crete and one on Corfu. Where else do you think I should visit?'

Giving her a grateful look, Diandra made several suggestions, but Nik refused to be deflected from his path.

'Who did you work for before my father?'

'Ignore him,' Lily said lightly. 'He makes every conversation feel like a job interview. The first time I met him I wanted to hand over my résumé. This lamb is *delicious* by the way. You're so clever. It's even better than the lamb Nik and I ate last week and that was a top restaurant.' She went on to describe what they'd eaten in minute detail and Diandra offered a few observations of her own about the best way to cook lamb.

Deprived of the opportunity to question his future stepmother further, Nik was wondering once again what 'news' his father was preparing to announce, when he heard the sound of a child crying inside the house.

Diandra shot to her feet and exchanged a brief look with his father before scurrying from the table.

Nik narrowed his eyes. 'Who,' he said slowly, 'is that?'

'That's the news I was telling you about.' His father turned his head and watched as Diandra returned to the table carrying a toddler whose tangled blonde curls and sleepy expression announced that she'd recently awoken from a nap. 'Callie has given me full custody of Chloe as a wedding present. Niklaus, meet your half-sister.'

CHAPTER SEVEN

LILY SAT ON the sunlounger in the shade, listening to the rhythmic splash from the infinity pool. Nik had been swimming for the past half an hour, with no break in the relentless laps back and forth across the pool.

Whatever had possessed her to agree to come for this wedding?

It had been like falling straight into the middle of a bad soap opera.

Diandra had been so intimidated by Nik she'd barely opened her mouth and he, it seemed, had taken that as a sign that she had nothing worth saying. Lunch had been a tense affair and the moment his father had produced his little half-sister Nik had gone from being coolly civil to remote and intimidating. Lily had worked so hard to compensate for his frozen silence she'd virtually performed cartwheels on the terrace.

And she couldn't comprehend his reaction.

He was too old to care about sharing the affections of his father, and too independently wealthy to care about the impact on his inheritance. The toddler was adorable, a cherub with golden curls and a ready smile, and his father and Diandra had been so obviously thrilled by the new addition to the family Lily couldn't understand the problem.

On the walk back from lunch she'd tentatively broached the subject but Nik had cut her off and made straight for his office where he'd proceeded to work without interruption.

Trying to cure her headache, Lily had drunk plenty of water and then read her book in the shade but she'd been unable to concentrate on the words.

She knew it was none of her business, but still she couldn't keep her mouth shut and when Nik finally vaulted from the pool in an athletic movement that displayed every muscle in his powerful frame, she slid off her sunlounger and blocked his path.

'You were horrible to Diandra at lunch and if you want to heal the rift with your father, that isn't the way. She is *not* a gold-digger.'

His face was an uncompromising mask. 'And you know this on less than a few minutes' acquaintance?'

'I'm a good judge of character.'

'This from a woman who didn't know a man was married?'

She felt herself flush. 'I was wrong about him, but I'm not wrong about Diandra, and you have to stop giving her the evil eye.'

Droplets of water clung to his bronzed shoulders. 'I was not giving her the evil eye.'

'Nik, you virtually grilled her at the table. I was waiting for you to throw her on the barbecue along with the lamb. You were terrifying.'

'*Theé mou,* that is *not* true. She behaved like a woman with a guilty conscience.'

'She behaved like a woman who was terrified of you! How can you be so *blind*?' And then she realised in a flash of comprehension that she was the one who was blind. He wasn't being small-minded, or prejudiced. That wasn't what was happening. She saw now that he was afraid for his father. His actions all stemmed from a desire to protect him. In his own way he was displaying the exact loyalty she valued so highly. Like a gazelle approaching a sleeping lion, she tiptoed carefully. 'I think your perspective may be a little skewed because of what happened with your father's other relationships. Do you want to talk about it?'

'Unlike you, I don't have the desire to verbalise every thought that enters my head.'

Lily stiffened. 'That was a little harsh given that I'm trying to help, but I'm going to forgive you because I can see you're very upset. And I think I know why.'

'Don't forgive me. If you're angry, say so.'

'You told me not to verbalise every thought that enters my head.'

Nik wiped his face with the towel and sent her a look that would have frozen molten lava. 'I don't need help.'

Lily tried a different approach. 'I can see that this situation has the potential for all sorts of complications, not least that Diandra has been given another woman's child to raise as her own just a few days before the wedding, but she seemed thrilled. Your father is clearly delighted. They're happy, Nik.'

'For how long?' His mouth tightened. 'How long until it all falls apart and his heart is broken again? What if this time he doesn't heal?' His words confirmed her suspicions and she felt a rush of compassion.

'This isn't about Diandra, it's about you. You love your father deeply and you're trying to protect him.' It was ironic, she thought, that Nik Zervakis, who was supposedly so cold and aloof, turned out to have stronger family values than

David Ashurst, who on the surface had seemed like perfect partner material. It was something that her checklist would never have shown up. 'I love that you care so much about him, but has it occurred to you that you might be trying to save him from the best thing that has ever happened in his life?'

'Why will this time be different from the others?'

'Because he loves her and she loves him. Of course having a toddler thrown into the mix will make for a challenging start to the relationship, but—' She frowned as she examined that fact in greater depth. 'Why did Callie choose to do this now? A child is a person, not a wedding present. You think she was hoping to derail your father's relationship with Diandra?'

'The thought had occurred to me but no, that isn't what she is trying to do.' He hesitated. 'Callie is marrying again and she doesn't want the child.'

He delivered that news in a flat monotone devoid of emotion, but this time Lily was too caught up in her own emotions to think about his.

Callie didn't want the child?

She felt as if she'd been punched in the gut. All the air had been sucked from her lungs and suddenly she couldn't breathe.

'Right.' Her voice was croaky. 'So she gives her up as if she's a dress that's gone out of fashion? I'm not surprised you didn't like her. She doesn't sound like a very likeable person.' Horrified by the intensity of her response and aware he was watching her closely, she moved past him. 'If you're sure you don't want to talk then I think I'm going to have a rest before dinner. The heat makes me sleepy.'

He frowned. 'Lily—'

'Dinner is at eight? I'll be ready by then.' She steered her shaky legs towards her bedroom and closed the door behind her.

What was the matter with her?

This wasn't her family.

It wasn't her life.

Why did she have to take everything so *personally*?

Why was she worrying about how little Chloe would feel when she was old enough to ask about her mother when it wasn't really any of her business? Why did she care about all the potential threats she could see to his family unit?

The door behind her opened and she stiffened but kept her back to him. 'I'm about to lie down.'

'I upset you,' he said quietly, 'and that was not my intention. You were generous enough to come here with me, the least I can do is respond to your questions in a civil tone. I apologise.'

'I'm not upset because you didn't want to talk. I understand you don't find it helpful.'

'Then what's wrong?' When she didn't reply he cursed softly. 'Talk to me, Lily.'

'No. I'm having lots of feelings of my own and you hate talking about feelings. And no doubt you'll find some way to interpret what I'm feeling in a bad way, because that seems to be your special gift. You twist everything beautiful into something dark and ugly. You really should leave now. I need to self-soothe.'

She expected to hear the pounding of feet and the sound of a door closing behind him, but instead felt the warm strength of his hands curve over her shoulders.

'I do not twist things.'

'Yes, you do. But that's your problem. I can't deal with it right now.'

'I don't want you to self-soothe.' The words sounded as if they were dragged from him. 'I want you to tell me what's wrong. My father asked you a lot of personal questions over lunch.'

'I don't mind that.'

'Then what? Is this about Chloe?'

She took a juddering breath. 'It's a little upsetting when adults don't consider how a child might feel. It's lovely that she has a loving father, but one day that little girl is going to wonder why her mother gave her away. She's going to ask herself whether she cried too much or did something wrong. Not that I expect you to understand.'

There was a long pulsing silence and his grip on her arms tightened. 'I do understand.' His voice was low. 'I was nine when my mother left and I asked myself all those questions and more.'

She stood still, absorbing both the enormity and the implications of that revelation. 'I didn't know.'

'I don't talk about it.'

But he'd talked about it now, with her. Warmth spread through her. 'Did seeing Chloe stir it all up for you?'

'This whole place stirs it up,' he said wearily. 'Let's hope Chloe doesn't ask herself those same questions when she's older.'

'I was a baby and I still ask myself those questions.' And she had questions for him, so many questions, but she knew they wouldn't be welcome.

'I appreciate you listening to me, but I know you don't really want to talk about this so you should probably leave now.'

'Seeing as I am indirectly responsible for the

fact you're upset by bringing you here in the first place, I have no intention of leaving.'

'You should.' Her voice was thickened. 'It's the situation, not you. You've never even met your half-sister so you can't be expected to love her and your father is obviously pleased, but a toddler is a lot of work and he's about to be married. What if he decides he doesn't want Chloe either?'

'He won't decide that.' His hands firm, he turned her to face him. 'He has wanted her from the first day, but Callie did everything she could to keep the child from him. I have no idea what my father will say when Chloe is old enough to ask, but he is a sensitive man—much more sensitive than I am as you have discovered—and he will say the right thing, I'm sure.' His hands stroked her bare arms and she gave a little shiver.

She could see the droplets of water clinging to dark hair that shadowed his bare chest.

Unable to help herself, she lifted her hand to his chest and then caught herself and pulled back.

'Sorry—' She took a step backwards but he muttered something under his breath in Greek and hauled her back against him. Her brain blurred as she was flattened against the heat and power of his body, his arm holding her trapped. He used his other hand to tilt her face to his and she drowned in the heated burn of his eyes in the few seconds before he bent his head and kissed her. And then there was nothing but the hunger of his mouth and the erotic slide of his tongue and it felt every bit as good as it had the first time. So good that she forgot everything except the pounding of her pulse and the desperate squirming heat low in her pelvis.

Pressed against his hard, powerful chest she forgot about feeling miserable and unsettled.

She forgot all the reasons this wasn't a good idea.

She forgot everything except the breathtaking excitement he generated with his mouth and hands. His kiss was unmistakably sexual, his tongue tangling with hers, his gaze locked on hers as he silently challenged her.

'Yes, yes.' With a soft murmur of acquiescence, she wrapped her arms round his neck, feeling the damp ends of his hair brush her wrists.

The droplets of water on his chest dampened her thin sundress until it felt as if there were nothing between them.

She felt him pull her hard against him, felt his hand slide down her back and cup her bottom so that she was pressed against the heavy thrust of his erection.

'I promised myself I wasn't going to do this but I want you.' He spoke in a thickened tone, and she gave a sob of relief.

'I want you, too. You have no idea how much. Right through lunch I wanted to rip your clothes off and remove that severe look from your face.'

He lifted his mouth from hers, his breathing uneven, the smouldering glitter of his eyes telling her everything she needed to know about his feelings. 'Do I look severe now?'

'No. You look incredible. This has been the longest week of my life.' She backed towards the bed, pulling him with her. If he changed his mind she was sure she'd explode. 'Don't have second thoughts. I know this is about sex and nothing else. I don't love you, but I'd love a repeat of all those things you did to me the other night.'

With sure hands, he dispensed with her sundress. 'All of them?'

'Yes.' She wanted him so badly it was almost indecent and when he lowered his head and trailed his mouth along her neck she almost sobbed aloud. 'Please. Right now. I want your whole repertoire. Don't hold anything back.'

'You're shy, it's still daylight,' he growled, 'and I don't have a blindfold.'

'I'm not shy. Shy has left the party. I don't care,

I don't care.' Her hands moved over his chest and lower to his damp swimming shorts. She struggled to remove them over the thrusting force of his erection but finally her frantic fumbling proved successful and she covered him with the flat of her hand.

He groaned low in his throat and tipped her onto the bed, covering her body with his, telling her how much he wanted her, how hard she made him, until the excitement climbed to a point where she was a seething, writhing mass of desire. She tore at his shirt with desperate hands and he swore under his breath and wrenched it over his head, his fingers tangling with hers.

'Easy, slow down, there's no rush.'

'Yes, there is.' She rolled him onto his back and pressed her mouth to the hard planes of his chest and lower until she heard him groan. She tried to straddle him but he flipped her onto her back and caught her shifting hips in his hands, anchoring her there.

Despite the simmering tension, there was laughter in his eyes. 'It would be a criminal waste to rush this, *theé mou.*'

'No, it wouldn't.' She slid her hands over the silken muscles of his back. 'It might kill me if you don't.'

It was hard to know which of them was most aroused. She saw it in the glitter of his eyes and heard it in his uneven breathing. Felt it in the slight shake of his fingers as he unhooked her bra and peeled it away from her, releasing her breasts, taking his time. Everything he did was slow, unhurried, designed to torture her and she wondered how he could exercise so much control, such brutal discipline, because if it had been up to her the whole thing would have been over by now. He kept her still with his weight, with soft words, with skilled kisses and the sensual slide of his hand that dictated both position and pace.

She felt the cool air from the ceiling fan brush the heated surface of her skin and then moaned aloud as he drew her into the dark heat of his mouth. Sensation was sweet and wild and she arched into him, only to find herself anchored firmly by the rough strength of his thigh. He worked his way down her body with slow exploratory kisses and she shivered as she felt the brush of his lips and the flick of his tongue. Lower, more intimate, his mouth wandered to the shadows between her thighs and she felt the slippery heat of his tongue opening her, tasting her until she could feel the pleasure thundering down on her. She was feverish, desperate, everything in her body centred on this one moment.

'Nik—I need—'

'I know what you need.' A brief pause and then he eased over her and into her, each driving thrust taking him deeper until she didn't know where she ended and he began and then he paused, his hand in her hair and his mouth against hers, eyes half closed as he studied her face. She was dimly aware that he was saying something, soft intimate words that blurred in her head and melted over her skin. She felt the delicious weight of him, the masculine invasion, the solidity of muscle, the scrape of his jaw against hers as he kissed her, murmured her name and told her all the things he wanted to do to her. And she moaned because she wanted him to do them, right now. He was controlling her but she didn't care because he knew things about her she didn't know herself. How to touch her, where to touch her. All she wanted was more of this breath-stealing pleasure and then he started to move, slowly at first, and then building the rhythm with sure, skilled thrusts until she was aware of nothing but him, of hard muscle and slick skin, of the frenzy of sensation until it exploded and she clung to him, sobbing his name as her body tightened on his, her muscles rippling around the thrusting length of him drawing out his own response.

She heard him groan her name, felt him slide his hand into her hair and take her mouth again so that they kissed their way through the whole thing, sharing every throb, ripple and flutter in the most intimate way possible.

The force of it left her shaken and stunned and she lay, breathless, trying to bring herself slowly back to earth. And then he shifted his weight and gathered her close, murmuring something in Greek as he stroked her hair back from her face and kissed her mouth gently.

They lay for a moment and then he scooped her up and carried her into the shower where, under the soft patter of steamy water, he proceeded to expand her sexual education with infinite skill until her body no longer felt like her own and her legs felt like rubber.

'Nik?' She lay damp and sated on the tangled sheets, deliciously sleepy and barely able to keep her eyes open. 'Is that why you don't like coming back here? Because it reminds you of your childhood?'

He stared down at her with those fathomless black eyes, his expression inscrutable. 'Get some sleep.' His voice was even. 'I'll wake you in time to change for dinner.'

'Where are you going?'

'I have work to do.'

In other words she'd strayed into forbidden territory. Somewhere in the back of her mind there was another question she wanted to ask him, but her brain was already drifting into blissful unconsciousness and she slid into a luxurious sleep.

Nik returned to the terrace and made calls in the shade, one eye on the open doors of Lily's bedroom.

So much for his resolve not to touch her again.

And what had possessed him to tell her about his mother? It was something he rarely thought about himself, let alone spoke of to other people.

It was being back here that had stirred up memories long buried.

He ignored the part of him that said it was the prospect of another wedding that stirred up the memories, not the place.

To distract himself he worked until the blaze of the sun dimmed and he heard movement from the bedroom.

He ended the call he'd made and a few minutes later she wandered onto the terrace, sleepy eyed and deliciously disorientated. 'Have you been out here the whole time?'

'Yes.'

'You're not tired?'

'No.'

'Because you're stressed out about your father.' She sat down next to him and poured herself a glass of water. 'For what it's worth, I like Diandra.'

He studied the soft curve of her mouth and the kindness in her eyes. 'Is there anyone you don't like?'

'Yes!' She sipped her water. 'I have a deep aversion to Professor Ashurst, and if we're drawing up a list then I should confess I didn't totally fall in love with your girlfriend from the other night, but that might be because she called me fat. And I definitely didn't like you a few hours ago, but you redeemed yourself in the bedroom so I'm willing to overlook the offensive things you said on the journey.' A dimple appeared in the corner of her mouth and Nik felt the instant, powerful response of his body and wondered how he was going to make it through an evening of small talk with people that didn't interest him.

She, on the other hand, interested him extremely.

'We should get ready for the party. The guests

will be arriving soon and my father wants us up there early to greet them.'

'Us? You, surely, not me.'

'He wants you, too. He likes you very much.'

'I like him, too, but I don't think I should be greeting his guests. I'm not family. We're not even together.' Her gaze slid to his and away again and he knew she was thinking about what they'd shared earlier.

He was, too. In fact he'd thought of little else but sex with Lily since she'd drenched herself in his shower a week earlier.

Sex had always been important to him, but since meeting her it had become an obsession.

'It would mean a lot to him if you were there.'

'Well, if you're sure that's what he wants. This all feels a bit surreal.'

'Which part feels surreal?'

'All of it. The whole rich-lifestyle thing. Living with you could turn a girl's head. You can snap your fingers and have anything you want.'

Relieved by the lightening of the atmosphere, he smiled. 'I will snap my fingers for you any time you like. Tell me what you want.'

She smiled. 'You can get me anything?'

'Anything.'

'So if I had a craving for lobster mousse, you'd find me one?'

'I would.' He reached for his phone and she covered his hand with hers, laughing.

'I wasn't serious! I don't want lobster mousse.' Her fingers were light on his hand. There was nothing suggestive about her touch. Nothing that warranted his extreme physical reaction.

'Then what?' His voice was husky. 'If you don't want lobster mousse, what can I get you?'

Her eyes met his and colour streaked across her cheeks. 'Nothing. I have everything I need.' She removed her hand quickly and said something, but her words were drowned out by the clacking of a helicopter.

Nik rose reluctantly to his feet. 'We need to move. The guests are arriving.'

'By helicopter?' Her eyes were round, as if it was only now dawning on her that this wasn't an ordinary wedding party. 'Is this party going to be glamorous?'

'Very. Lunch was an informal family affair, but tonight is for my father to show off his new wife.'

'How many guests?'

'A very select party. No more than two hundred, but they're arriving from all over Europe and the US.'

'Two *hundred*? That's a select party?' Her smile faltered. 'I'm a gatecrasher.'

'You are not a gatecrasher. You're my guest.'

She pushed her hair back from her face. 'I'm starting to panic that what I brought with me isn't dressy enough.'

'You look lovely in everything you wear, but I do have something if you'd like to take a look at it.'

'Something you bought for someone else?'

'No. For you.'

'I told you I didn't want anything.'

'I didn't listen.'

'So you bought me something anyway. In case I embarrassed you?'

'No. In case you had a panic that what you'd brought wasn't dressy enough.'

'I should probably be angry that you're calling me predictable, but as we don't have time to be angry I'm going to overlook it. Can I see?' She stood up at the same time he did and her body brushed against his.

'Lily…' He breathed her name, steadied her with his hands and she gave a low moan.

'No.' Her eyes were clouded. 'Seriously, Nik, if we do it again I'll fall asleep and never wake up.

The Prince is supposed to wake Sleeping Beauty, not put her to sleep with endless sex.'

He lifted his hand to her flushed cheek and gently stroked her hair back from her face. It took all his will power not to power her back against the wall. 'We could skip the party. Better still, we could grab a couple of bottles of champagne and have our own party here by the pool.'

'No way! Not only would that upset your father and Diandra, but I wouldn't get to ogle all those famous people. Brittany will grill me later so I need to have details. Am I allowed to take photographs?'

'Of course.' With a huge effort of will he let his hand drop. 'You'd better try the dress.'

The dress was exquisite. A long sheath of shimmering turquoise silk with delicate beads handsewn around the neckline. It fitted her perfectly.

She picked up her phone, took a quick selfie and sent it to Brittany with a text saying Rebound sex is my new favourite thing.

People were wrong when they thought rebound sex didn't involve any emotion, she mused. Yes, the sex was spectacular, but even though she wasn't in love that didn't mean two people couldn't care about each other. She cared about making this wedding as easy as possible for Nik, and he'd cared enough not to leave her alone when she was upset.

Somewhere deep inside a small part of her wondered if perhaps that wasn't how she was supposed to be feeling, but she dismissed it, picked up her purse and walked through to the living room.

'I could be a little freaked out by how well you're able to guess my size.'

He turned, sleek and handsome in a dinner suit.

Despite the undisputable elegance and sophistication, formal dress did nothing to disguise the lethal power of the man beneath.

Testosterone in a tux, she thought as he reached into his pocket and handed her something.

'What's this?' She took the slim, elegant box and opened it cautiously. There, nestled in deep blue velvet, was a necklace of silver and sapphire she immediately recognised. 'It's one of Skylar's. I admired the picture.'

'And now you can admire the real thing. I thought it would look better on your neck than in a catalogue.' He took it from her and fastened it round her neck while she pressed her fingers to her throat self-consciously.

'When did you buy this?'

'I had it flown in after you admired her pot.'

'You had it *flown in*? From New York? There wasn't time.'

'This piece was in a gallery in London.'

'Unbelievable. So extravagant.'

'Then why are you smiling?'

'Because I like pretty things and Skylar makes the prettiest things.' Smiling, she pulled her phone out of her purse again. 'I need to capture the moment so when I'm sitting in my pyjamas in a cramped apartment in rainy London I can re-live this moment. It's a loan, obviously, because I could never accept a gift this generous.' She took a couple of photos and then made him pose with her. 'I promise not to sell these to the newspapers. Can I send it to Sky? I can say *Look what I'm wearing.*'

A smile touched the corners of his mouth. 'It's your photo. You can do anything you like with it.'

'Skylar will be over the moon. I'm going to make sure everyone sees this necklace tonight. Now, tell me how you're feeling.' She'd asked herself over and over again if his earlier confession was something she should mention or not. But how could she ignore it when it was clearly the source of his stress?

His expression shifted from amused to guarded. 'How I'm feeling?'

'This is a party to celebrate your father's impending wedding, which you didn't want to attend. Is it hard to be here thinking about your mother and watching your father marry again? It must make marriage seem like a disposable object.'

'I appreciate your concern, but I'm fine.'

'Nik, I know you're not fine, but if you'd rather not talk about it—'

'I'd rather not talk about it.'

She kept her thoughts on that to herself. 'Then let's go.' She slipped her hand into his. 'I guess everyone will be trying to work out whether you're pleased or not, so for Diandra's sake make sure you smile.'

'Thank you for your counsel.'

'Ouch, that was quite a put-down. I presume that was your way of telling me to stop talking.'

'If I want to stop you talking, I have more effective methods than a verbal put-down.'

She caught his eye. 'If you feel like testing out one of those methods, go right ahead.'

'Don't tempt me.'

She was shocked by how badly she wanted to tempt him. She considered dragging him back inside, but a car was waiting outside the villa for them. 'I didn't realise there were cars on the island. How do they get across here?'

'There is a ferry, but my father usually takes a helicopter to the mainland if he is travelling.'

'We could have walked tonight.'

'There is no way you'd be able to walk that far in those shoes, let alone dance.'

'Who says I'll be dancing?'

His gaze slid to hers. 'I do.'

'You seem very sure of that.'

'I am, because you'll be dancing with me.'

She felt a shiver of excitement, excitement that grew as they drew up outside the imposing main entrance. The villa was situated on the far side of the island, out of sight of the mainland. 'This is a mansion, not a villa. Normal people don't live like this.'

'You think I'm not a normal person?'

'I *know* you're not.' She took his arm as they walked past a large fountain to the floodlit entrance of the villa. 'Normal people don't own five homes and a private jet.'

'The jet is owned by the company.'

'And you own the company.' It was hard not to feel overwhelmed as she walked through the door into the palatial entrance of his father's home. Towering ceilings gave a feeling of space and light and through open doors she caught a glimpse of rooms tastefully furnished with antiques and fine art. 'Tell me again what your father does?'

Nik smiled. 'He ran a very successful company, which he sold for a large sum of money.'

'But not to you.'

'Our interests are different.'

There was no opportunity for him to elaborate because Diandra was hovering and Lily noticed the nervous look she gave Nik.

To break the ice, she enthused over the other woman's dress and hair and then asked after Chloe.

'She's sleeping. My niece is watching her while we greet everyone, then I'm going to check on her. It's been a very unsettling time.' Diandra kept her voice low. 'I wanted to postpone the wedding but Kostas won't hear of it.'

'You're right, I won't.' Kostas took Diandra's hand. 'Nothing is going to stop me marrying you. You worry too much. She will soon settle and in the meantime we have an army of staff to attend to her happiness.'

'She doesn't need an army,' Diandra murmured. 'She needs the security of a few people she knows and trusts.'

'We'll discuss this later.' Kostas drew her closer.

'Our guests are arriving. Lily, you look beautiful. You will stand with us and greet everyone.'

'Oh, but I—'

'I insist.'

Lily quickly discovered that Nik's father was as skilled at getting his own way as his son.

Unable to extract herself, she stood and greeted the guests, feeling as if she were on a movie set as a wave of shimmering, glittering guests flowed past her.

'This isn't my life,' she whispered to Nik but he simply smiled and exchanged a few words with each guest, somehow managing to make everyone feel as if they'd had his full attention.

She discovered that even among this group of influential people everyone wanted a piece of him, especially the women.

It gave her a brief but illuminating insight into his life and she saw how it must be for him, surrounded by people whose motives in wanting to know him were as mixed up and murky as the bottom of the ocean.

She was beginning to understand both his reserve and his cynicism.

The evening was like something out of a dream, except that none of her dreams had ever featured an evening as glittering and extravagant as this.

What would it be like, she wondered, if this really *were* her life?

She pushed that thought aside quickly, preferring not to linger in fantasyland. Wanting a family was one thing, this was something else altogether.

Candles flickered, silverware gleamed and the air was filled with the heady scent of expensive perfume and fresh flowers. The food, a celebration of all things Greek, was served on the terrace so that the guests could enjoy the magnificent sight of the sun setting over the Aegean.

By the time Nik finally swung her onto the dance floor Lily was dizzy with it.

'I talked to a few people while you were in conversation with those men in suits. I didn't mention the fact I'm a penniless archaeologist.'

'Are you enjoying yourself?'

'What do you think?'

'I think you look stunning in that dress.' He eased her closer. 'I also think you are better at mindless small talk than I am.'

'Are you calling me mindless?' She rested her hand lightly on his chest. 'Did you know that the very good-looking man over there with the lovely wife owns upmarket hotels all over the world? He's Sicilian.'

He glanced over her shoulder. 'Cristiano Ferrara? You think he's good-looking?'

'Yes. And his wife is beautiful. They seem like a happy family.'

He smiled. 'Her name is Laurel.'

'Do you know everyone? She was very down-to-earth. She admired my necklace and he pulled me to one side to ask me for the details. He's going to surprise her for her birthday.'

'If Skylar sells a piece of jewellery to a Ferrara I can assure you she's made. They move in the highest circles.'

'Laurel wants an invitation to her exhibition in London. I have plugged Skylar's jewellery to at least ten *very* wealthy people. I hope you're not angry.'

He curved her against him in a possessive gesture. 'You are welcome to be as shameless as you wish. In fact I'm willing to make a few specific suggestions about how you could direct that shameless behaviour.'

A few heads turned in their direction.

'Thank you for telling this room full of strangers that I'm a sex maniac. Are you sure you don't want to dance with someone else?'

His eyes were half shut, his gaze focused entirely on her. 'Why would I want to dance with anyone else?'

'Because there are a lot of women in this room and they're looking at you hopefully. Me, they look as if they'd like to kill. They're wondering why you're with me.'

'None of the men are wondering that,' he drawled. 'Trust me on that.'

'Can I tell you something?'

'That depends. Is it going to be a deeply emotional confession that is going to send me running from the room?'

'You can't run anywhere because your father is about to make a speech and—oh—' she frowned '—Diandra looks stressed.' Taking his hand, she tugged him across the crowded dance floor towards Diandra, who appeared to be arguing with Kostas.

'Wait five minutes,' Kostas urged in a low tone. 'You cannot abandon our guests.'

'But she needs me,' Diandra said firmly and Lily intervened.

'Is this about Chloe?'

'She's woken up. I can't bear to think of her upset with people she doesn't know. It's already hard enough on her to have been left here by her mother.'

'Nik and I will go to her,' Lily said immediately and saw Nik frown.

'I don't think—'

'We'll be fine. Make your speech and then come and find us.' Without letting go of Nik's hand, Lily made for the stairs. 'I assume you know where the nursery is or should we use GPS?'

'I really don't think—'

'Cut the excuses, Zervakis. Your little sister needs you.'

'She doesn't know me. I don't see how my sudden appearance in her life can do anything but make things a thousand times worse.'

'Children are sometimes reassured by a strong presence. But stop glaring.' She paused at the top of the stairs. 'Which way?'

He sighed and led the way up another flight of stairs to a suite of rooms and pushed open the door.

A young girl stood there jiggling a red-faced crying toddler. Relief spread across her features when she saw reinforcements.

'She's been like this for twenty minutes. I can't stop her crying.'

Nik took one look at the abject misery on his half-sister's face and took her from the girl, but, instead of her being comforted by the reassuring strength in those arms, Chloe's howls intensified.

Sending Lily a look that said 'I told you so', he immediately handed her over.

'Perhaps you can do a better job than I can.'

She was about to point out that he was a stranger and that Chloe's response was no reflection on him when the toddler flopped onto her shoulder, exhausted.

'You poor thing,' Lily soothed. 'Did you wake and not know where you were? Was it noisy downstairs?' She continued to talk, murmuring soothing nothings and stroking the child's back until the child's eyelids drifted closed. She felt blonde curls tickle her chin. 'There, that's better, you must be exhausted. Are you thirsty? Would you like a drink?' She glanced across the room and saw Nik watching her, his expression inscrutable. 'Say something.'

'What do you want me to say?'

'Something. Anything. You look as if someone has released a tiger from a cage and you're expected to bag it single-handed.'

There was a tension in his shoulders that hadn't been there a few moments earlier and suddenly she wondered if his response to the child was mixed up with his feelings for Callie.

It was obvious he'd disliked his father's third wife, but surely he wouldn't allow those feelings to extend to the child?

And then she realised he wasn't looking at Chloe, he was looking at her.

He lifted his hand and loosened his tie with a few flicks of those long, bronzed fingers. 'You love children.'

'Well I don't love *all* children, obviously, but at this age they're pretty easy to love.' She waited for him to walk across the room and take his sister from her, but he didn't move. Instead he leaned against the doorway, watching her, and then finally eased himself upright.

'You seem to have this under control.' His voice was level. 'I'll see you downstairs when you're ready.'

'No! Nik, wait—' She shifted Chloe onto her other hip and walked across to him, intending to hand over the wriggling toddler so that he could form a bond with her, but he took a step back, his face a frozen mask.

'I'll send Diandra up as soon as she's finished with the speeches.' With that he turned and strode out of the room leaving her holding the baby.

CHAPTER EIGHT

NIK MADE HIS way through the guests, out onto the terrace and down past the cascading water feature that ended in a beautiful pool. Children cried for a million reasons, he knew that, but that didn't stop him wondering if deep down Chloe knew her mother had abandoned her. The fact that he'd been unable to offer comfort had done nothing for his elevated stress levels, but the real source of his tension had been the look on Lily's face.

He could see now he'd made a huge mistake bringing her here. *Cristos*, who was he kidding? The mistake had been taking her back to his place from the restaurant that night, instead of dropping her safely at her apartment and telling her to lock the door behind her.

She was completely, totally wrong for him and he was completely, totally wrong for her.

Cursing under his breath, he yanked off his tie and ran his hand over his jaw.

'Nik?'

Her voice came from behind him and he turned to find her standing there, her sapphire eyes gleaming bright in the romantic light of the pool area. The turquoise dress hugged the lush lines of her body and her blonde hair, twisted into Grecian braids, glowed like a halo. The jewel he'd given her sat at the base of her throat and suddenly all he wanted to do was rip it off and replace it with his mouth. There wasn't a man in the room who hadn't taken a second glance at her and he was willing to bet she hadn't noticed. He'd always considered jealousy to be a pointless and ugly emotion but tonight he'd experienced it in spades. He should have given her a dress of shapeless black, although he had a feeling that would have made no difference to the way he felt. It was a shock to discover that will power alone wasn't enough to hold back the brutal arousal.

'I thought you were with Chloe. Is she asleep?'

'Diandra came to take over. And you shouldn't have walked away from her.' She was stiff. Furious, displaying none of the softness and gentleness he'd witnessed in the nursery.

The wind had picked up and he frowned as he saw her shiver and run her hands over her arms. 'Are you cold? Crete often experiences high winds.'

'I'm not cold. I'm being heated from the inside out because I'm boiling mad, Nik. I don't think it's exactly fair of you to take your feelings for her mother out on a child, that's all.'

Nik took a deep breath, wondering how honest to be. 'That is not what is happening here.'

'No? Well there has to be some reason why you looked at Chloe as if she was a dangerous animal.'

'This is not about Chloe.'

'What then?'

There was a long, throbbing pause. 'It's about you.'

'Me?' She stared at him blankly and he cursed under his breath.

'You are the sort of woman who cannot pass a baby without wanting to pick it up. You see sunshine in a thunderstorm, happy endings everywhere you look and you believe family is the answer to every problem in the world.'

She stared at him with a total lack of comprehension. 'I do like babies, that's true, and I don't see any reason to apologise for the fact I'd like a family one day. I don't see sunshine in every thunderstorm, but I do try and see the positive rather than the negative because that's how I prefer to live my life. I put up an umbrella instead of standing there and getting wet. Sometimes life can be crap, I know that but I've learned not to focus on the crap and I won't apologise for that. But I don't see what that has to do with the situation. None of that explains why you behaved the way you did in that room. You looked as if you'd been hit round the head with a plank of wood and then you walked out. And you say it was about me, but how can it possibly—?'

Her expression changed, the shards of anger in her eyes changing to wariness. 'Oh. I get it. You're worried that because I want a family one day, that because I like babies, it makes me a dangerous person to have sex with, is that right?' She spoke slowly, feeling it out, watching his face the whole time and she must have seen something there that confirmed her suspicions because she made a derisive sound and turned away.

'Lily—'

'No! Don't make excuses or find a tactful way to express how you feel. It's sprayed over you like graffiti.' She hitched up her dress and started to walk away from him and he gritted his teeth because he could see she was truly upset.

'Wait. You can't walk back in those shoes—'

'Of course I can. What do you think I usually do when I'm out? I'd never been in a limo in my life before I met you. I walk everywhere because it's cheaper.' She hurled the words over her shoulder and he strode after her, wondering how to intervene and prevent a broken ankle without stoking her wrath.

'We should talk about this—'

'There is nothing to talk about.' She didn't slacken her pace. 'I cuddled your baby sister and you're afraid that somehow changed our relationship. You're worried that this isn't about sex any more, and that I've suddenly fallen in love with you. Your arrogance is shocking.'

He kept pace with her, ready to catch her if she twisted her ankle in those shoes. 'It is not arrogance. But that incident upstairs reinforced how different we are.'

'Yes, we're different. That's why I picked you for my rebound guy. It's true I want children one day, but believe me you're the last man on earth I'd want to share that with. I don't want a guy who describes a crying child as an "incident".'

'That is not—*Cristos,* will you *stop* for a moment?' He caught her arm and she shrugged him off, turning to face him.

'Believe me, Nik, I have never been *less* likely to fall in love with you than I am right at this moment. A little girl was distressed and all you could think about was how to extract yourself from a relationship you're not even having! That doesn't make you a great catch in my eyes so you're perfectly safe. I understand now why you have emotionless relationships. You're brilliant at the mechanics of sex, but that's it. I'd get as much emotional comfort from a laptop. Seriously, you should stick to your technology, or your investments or whatever it is you do—' She tugged her arm from his grip and carried on walking down the path, her distress evident in each furious tap of her heels.

He stared after her, stunned into silence by her unexpected attack and shaken by his own feelings. In emotional terms, he kept women at a distance. He'd never aspired to a deeper attachment and when his relationships ended he invariably felt nothing. He had no interest in marriage and didn't care about long-term commitment.

But he really, really cared that Lily was upset.

The feeling was uncomfortable, like having a stone in his shoe.

He followed at a safe distance, relieved when she reached the terrace and ripped off her shoes. She dumped them unceremoniously on a sun-lounger and carried on walking. The braids of her Grecian goddess hairstyle had been loosened by the wind, and her hair slithered in tumbled curls over her bare shoulders.

A man with a sense of self-preservation would have left her to cool down.

Nik carried on walking. He walked right into the bedroom, narrowly avoiding a black eye as she swung the door closed behind her.

He caught it on the flat of his hand, strode through and slammed it shut behind him.

She turned, her eyes a furious blaze of blue. 'Get out, Nik.'

He shrugged off his jacket and slung it over the nearest chair. 'No.'

'You should, because the way I feel right now I might punch you. No, wait a minute, I know exactly how to make you back out of that door.' She tilted her head and her mouth curved into a smile that didn't reach her eyes. 'You should leave, Nik, because I'm—oh, seconds away from falling in love with your irresistible self.' Her sarcasm made him smile and that smile was like throwing petrol on flame. 'Are you laughing at me?'

'No, I'm smiling because you're cute when you're angry.'

'I'm not cute. I'm fearsome and terrifying.'

What was fearsome and terrifying was how much he wanted her but he kept that thought to himself as he strolled towards her. 'Can we start this conversation again?'

'There is nothing more to say. Stop right there, Nik. Don't take another step.'

He kept walking. 'I should not have left you with Chloe. I behaved like an idiot, I admit it,' he breathed, 'but I'm not used to having a relationship with a woman like you.'

'And you're afraid I don't understand the rules? Trust me, I not only understand them but I applaud them. I wouldn't *want* to fall in love with someone like you. You make Neanderthal man look progressive and I've studied Neanderthal man. And stop looking at me like that because there is no way I can have sex with you when I'm this angry. It's not happening, Nik. Forget it.'

He stopped toe to toe with her, slid his hand into her hair and tilted her face to his. 'You've never had angry sex?'

'Of course not! Until you, I've only ever had "in love" sex. Angry sex sounds horrible. Sex should be loving and gentle. Who on earth would want to—?' Her words died as he silenced her with his mouth.

He cupped her face, feeling the softness of her skin beneath his fingers and the frantic beat of her pulse. He took her mouth with a hunger bordering on aggression and felt her melt against him. Her arms sneaked round his neck and he explored the sweet heat of her mouth, so aroused he was ready to rip off her dress and play out any one of the explicit scenarios running through his brain.

He had no idea what it was about her that attracted him so much, but right now he wouldn't have cared if she was holding an armful of babies and singing the wedding march, he still would have wanted to get her naked.

Without lifting his mouth from hers, he hauled her dress up to her waist and slid his fingers inside the lace of her panties. He heard her moan, felt her slippery hot and ready for him, and then her hands were on his zip, fumbling as she tried desperately to free him. As her cool fingers closed around him his mind blanked. He powered her back against the wall, slid his hands under her thighs and lifted her easily, wrapping her legs around his hips.

'Nik—' She sobbed his name against his mouth, dug her nails into his shoulders and he anchored her writhing hips with his hands and thrust deep. Gripped by tight, velvet softness, he felt his vision blur. Control was so far from his reach he abandoned hope of ever meeting up again and simply surrendered to the out-of-control desire that seemed to happen whenever he was near this woman.

He withdrew and thrust again, bringing thick waves of pleasure cascading down on both of them. From that moment on there was nothing but the wildness of it. He felt her nails digging into his shoulders and the frantic shifting of her hips. He tried to slow things down, to still those sensuous movements, but they were both out of control and he felt the first powerful ripples of her body clenching his shaft.

'*Cristo*—' He gave a deep, throaty groan and tried to hold back but there was no holding back and he surrendered to a raw explosive climax that wiped his mind of everything except this woman.

It was only when he lowered her unsteadily to the floor that he realised he was still dressed.

He couldn't remember when he'd last had sex fully clothed.

Usually he had more finesse, but finesse hadn't been invited to this party.

He felt her sway slightly and curved a protective arm around her, supporting her against him. His cheek was on her hair and he could feel the rise and fall of her chest as she struggled for air.

Finally she locked her hand in the front of his shirt and lifted her head. Her mouth was softly swollen and pink from his kisses, her eyes dazed. 'That was angry sex?'

Nik was too stunned to answer and she gave a faint smile and gingerly let go of the front of his shirt, as if testing her ability to stand unsupported.

'Angry sex is good. I don't feel angry any more. You've taught me a whole new way of solving a row.' She swayed like Bambi and he caught her before she could slide to the floor.

'*Theé mou*, you are *not* going to use sex to solve a row.' The thought of her doing with anyone else what she'd done with him sent his stress levels soaring.

'You did. It worked. I'm not saying I like you, but all my adrenaline was channelled in a different direction so I'm feeling a lot calmer. My karma is calmer.'

Nik was far from calm. 'Lily—'

'I know this whole thing is difficult for you,' she said, 'and you don't need to make the situation more difficult by worrying about me falling in love with you. That is never going to happen. And next time your little sister is upset, don't hand her to someone else. I know you don't like tears, but I think you could make an exception for a distressed two-year-old. Man up.'

Nik, who had never before in his life had his

manhood questioned, struggled for a response. 'She needed comfort and I have zero experience with babies.' He spoke through his teeth. 'My approach to all problems is to delegate tasks to whichever person has the superior qualifications—in this instance it was you. She liked you. She was calmer with you. With me, she cried.'

She gave him a look that was blisteringly unsympathetic. 'Every expert started as a beginner. Get over yourself. Next time, pick her up and learn how to comfort her. Who knows, one day you might even be able to extend those skills to grown-ups. If you didn't find it so hard to communicate you might not have gone so long without seeing your father. He adores you, Nik, and he's so proud of you. I know you didn't like Callie, but couldn't you have swallowed your dislike of her for the occasional visit? Would that really have been so hard?'

Nik froze. 'You know nothing about the situation.' Unaccustomed to explaining his actions to anyone, he took a deep breath. 'I did *not* stay away from my father because of my feelings about Callie.'

'What then?'

He was silent for a long moment because it was a topic he had never discussed with anyone. 'I stayed away from him because of her feelings for me.'

'That's what I'm saying! Because the two of you didn't get along, he suffered.'

'Not because I didn't like her. Because she liked me—a little too much.' He spoke with raw emphasis and saw the moment her expression changed and understanding dawned. 'That's right. My stepmother took her desire to be "close" to me to disturbing extremes.'

Lily's expression moved through a spectrum encompassing confusion, disbelief and finally horror. 'Oh, *no*, your poor father—does he know?'

'I sincerely hope not. I stayed away to avoid there ever being any chance he would witness something that might cause him distress. Despite my personal views on Callie I did not wish to see his marriage ended and I certainly didn't want to be considered the cause of it, because that would have created a rift that never would have healed.'

'So you stayed away to prevent a rift between you, but it caused a rift anyway and he doesn't even know the reason. Do you think you should have told him?'

'I asked myself that question over and over again, but I decided not to.' He hesitated. 'She was unfaithful several times during their short marriage and my father knew. There was nothing to be gained by revealing the truth and I didn't want to add to my father's pain.'

'Of course you didn't.' Lily's eyes filled. 'And all this time I was thinking it was because of your stubborn pride, because you didn't like the woman and were determined to punish him. I was *so wrong*. I'm sorry. Please forgive me.'

More unsettled by the tears than he was by her anger, Nik backed away. 'Don't cry. And there is nothing to forgive you for.'

'I misjudged you. I leaped to conclusions and I try never to do that.'

'It doesn't matter.'

'It does to me. You said that she had affairs—' Her eyes widened. 'Do you think that Chloe might not be—?'

He tensed because it was a possibility that had crossed his mind. 'I don't know, but it makes no difference now. My father's lawyers are taking steps to make sure it's a legal adoption.'

'But if she isn't and your father ever finds out—'

'It would make no difference to the way he feels about Chloe. Despite everything, I actually do believe she is my father's child. For a start she has certain physical characteristics that are particular to my family, and then there is the fact that Callie did everything in her power to keep her from him.'

'You really think she used her child as currency?'

'Yes.' Nik didn't hesitate and he saw the distress in her eyes.

'I think I dislike her almost as much as you do.'

'I doubt that.'

'I'm starting to see why you were worried about your father marrying again. Is Callie the reason you don't believe love exists?'

'No.' His voice didn't sound like his own. 'I formed that conclusion long before Callie.'

He waited for her to question him further but instead she leaned forward and hugged him tightly.

Unaccustomed to any physical contact that wasn't sexual, he tensed. 'What's that for?'

'Because you were put in a hideous, *horrible* position with Callie and the only choice you had was to stay away from your father. I think you're a very honourable person.'

He breathed deeply. 'Lily—'

'And because you were let down by a woman at a very vulnerable age. But I know you don't want to talk about that so I won't mention it again. And now why don't we go to bed and have apology sex? That's one we haven't tried before, but I'm willing to give it my all.'

Hours later they lay on top of the bed, wrapped around each other while the night breeze cooled their heated flesh.

Lily thought he was asleep, but then he stirred and tightened his grip.

'Thank you for helping with Chloe. You were very good with her.'

'One day I'd love to have children of my own, but it isn't something I usually admit to out loud. When people ask about your aspirations, they want to hear about your career. Wanting a family isn't a valid life choice. And I'm happy and interested in my job, but I don't want it to be all there is in my life.'

'Why did you choose archaeology?'

'I suppose I'm fascinated by the way people lived in the past. It tells us a lot about where we come from. Maybe it's because I don't know where I come from that it always interested me.'

There was a long silence. 'You know nothing about your mother?'

'Very little. I like to think she loved me, but she wasn't able to care for me. We assume she was a teenager. What I always wonder is why no one helped her. She obviously didn't feel she could even tell anyone she was pregnant. I think about that more than anything and I feel horrible that there wasn't anyone special in her life she could trust. She must have been so lonely and frightened.'

'Have you tried to trace her?'

'The police tried to trace her at the time but they had no success. They thought she was probably from somewhere outside London.' It was something she hadn't discussed with anyone before and she wondered why she was doing so now, with him. Maybe because he, too, had been abandoned by his mother, even though the circumstances were different. Or maybe because his honesty made him surprisingly easy to talk to. He didn't sugar coat his views on life, nor did he lie. After the brutal shock of discovering how wrong she'd been about David Ashurst, it was a relief to be with someone who was exactly who he seemed to be. And although she'd accused Nik of arrogance, part of her could understand how watching her with Chloe might have unsettled him. That moment had highlighted their basic differences and the truth was that his extreme reaction to her 'baby moment' had been driven more by his reluctance to mislead her, than arrogance.

It was obvious that his issues with love and marriage had been cemented early in life.

What psychological damage had his mother caused when she'd walked out leaving her young son watching from the hallway?

What message had that sent to him? That relationships didn't last? If a mother could leave her child, what did that say to a young boy about the enduring quality of love?

He'd been let down by the one person he should have been able to depend on, his childhood rocked by insecurity and lack of trust. Everything that had followed had cemented his belief that relationships were a transitory thing with no substance.

'We're not so different, you and I, Nik Zervakis.' She spoke softly. 'We're each a product of our pasts, except that it sent us in different directions. You ceased to believe true love existed, whereas I was determined to find it. It's why we're both bad at relationships.'

'I'm not bad at relationships.'

'You don't have relationships, Nik. You have sex.'

'Sex is a type of relationship.'

'Not really. It's superficial.'

'Why are we talking about me? Tell me why you think you're bad at relationships.'

'Because I care too much. I try too hard.'

'You want the fairy tale.'

'Not really. When you describe it that way it makes it sound silly and unachievable and I don't think what I want is unrealistic.'

'What do you want?'

There was a faint splash from beyond the open doors as a tiny bird skimmed across the pool.

'I want to be special to someone.' She spoke softly, saying the words aloud for the first time in her life. 'Not just special. I'm going to tell you something, and if you laugh you will be sorry—'

'I promise not to laugh.'

'I want to be someone's favourite person.'

There was a long silence and then his arms tightened. 'I'm sure you're special to a lot of people.'

'Not really.' She felt the hot sting of tears and was relieved it was dark. 'My life has been like a car park. People come and go. No one stays around for long. I have friends. Good friends, but it's not the same as being someone's favourite person. I want to be someone's dream come true. I want to be the person they call when they're happy or sad. The one they want to wake up next to and grow old with.' She wondered why she was telling him this, when his ambitions were diametrically opposed to hers. 'You think I'm crazy.'

'That isn't what I think.' His voice was husky and she turned her head to look at him but his features were indistinct in the darkness.

'Thank you for listening.' She felt sleep descend and suppressed a yawn. 'I know you don't think love exists, but I hope that one day you find a favourite person.'

'In bed, you are definitely my favourite person. Does that count?' He pulled the sheet up over her body, but didn't release her. 'Now get some sleep.'

The next couple of days passed in a whirl of social events. Helicopters and boats came and went, although tucked away on the far side of the idyllic island Lily was barely aware of the existence of other people. For her, it was all about Nik.

There had been a subtle shift in their relationship, although she had a feeling that the shift was all on her side. Now, instead of believing him to be cold and aloof, she saw that he was guarded. Instead of controlling, she saw him as someone determined to be in charge of his own destiny.

In between socialising, she lounged by the pool and spent time on the small private beach next to Camomile Villa.

She loved swimming in the sea and more than once Nik had to extract her with minutes to spare before she was expected to accompany him to another lunch or dinner.

He was absent a lot of the time and she was aware that he'd been spending that time with his father and, judging from the more harmonious atmosphere, that time had been well spent.

After that first awkward lunch, he'd stopped firing questions at Diandra and if he wasn't completely warm in his interactions with her, he was at least civil.

To avoid the madness of the wedding preparations, Nik was determined to show Lily the island.

The day before the wedding he pulled her from bed just before sunrise.

'What time do you call this?' Sleepy and fuzzy-headed after a night that had consisted of more sex than sleep, she grumbled her way to the bathroom and whimpered a protest when he thrust her under cold water. 'You're a sadist.'

'You are going to thank me. Wear sturdy shoes.'

'The Prince never said that to Cinderella and I am never going to thank you for anything.' But she dragged on her shorts and a pair of running shoes, smothering a yawn as she followed him out of the villa. She stopped when she saw the vintage Vespa by the gates. 'I hate to be the one to tell you this but something weird happened to your limo overnight.'

'When I was a teenager this was my favourite way of getting round the island.' He swung his leg over the bike with fluid predatory grace and she laughed.

'You are too tall for this thing.' But her heart gave a little bump as she slid behind him and wrapped her arms round hard male muscle. 'Shouldn't I have a helmet or a seat belt or something?'

'Hold onto me.'

They wound their way along dusty roads, past rocky coves and beautiful beaches and up to the crumbling ruins of the Venetian fort where they abandoned the scooter and walked the rest of the way. He took her hand and they scrambled to the top as dawn was breaking.

The view was breathtaking, and she sat next to him, her thigh brushing his as they watched the sun slowly wake and stretch out fingers of dazzling light across the surface of the sea.

'I could live here,' she said simply. 'There's something about the light, the warmth, the people—London seems so grey in comparison. I can't believe you grew up here. You're so lucky. Not that you know that of course—you take it all for granted.'

'Not all.'

He'd brought a flask of strong Greek coffee and some of the sweet pastries she adored and she nibbled the corner and licked her fingers.

'I don't believe you made those.'

'Diandra made both the coffee and the pastries.'

'Diandra.' She grinned and nudged him with her shoulder. 'Confess. You're starting to like her.'

'She is an excellent cook.'

'And a good person. You're starting to like her.'

'I admit that what I took for a guilty conscience appears to be shyness.'

'You like her.'

His eyes gleamed. 'Maybe. A little.'

'There, you said it and it didn't kill you. I'll make a romantic of you yet.' She finished the pastry, contemplated another and decided she wouldn't get into the dress she'd brought to wear at the wedding. 'That was the perfect start to the day.'

'Worth waking up for?' His voice was husky and she turned her head, met his sleepy, sexy gaze and felt her tummy tumble.

'Yes. Of course, it would be easier to wake up if you'd let me sleep at night.'

He lowered his forehead to hers. 'Do you want to sleep, *erota mou*?' He curved his hand behind her head and kissed her with lingering purpose. 'I could take you back to bed right now if that is what you want.'

Her heart was pounding. She had to keep telling herself that this was about sex and nothing else. 'What's the alternative?'

'There are Minoan remains west of here if you want to extend the trip.'

'There are Minoan remains all over Crete,' she said weakly, telling herself that she could spend the rest of her life digging around in Minoan remains, but after this trip was over she'd never again get the chance to spend time with Nik Zervakis. 'Bed sounds good to me.'

CHAPTER NINE

THE CREAM OF Europe's great and good turned up to witness the wedding of Kostas Zervakis and Diandra.

'It's busier than Paris in fashion week,' Lily observed as they gathered for the actual wedding.

Nik was looking supremely handsome in a dark suit and whatever reservations he had about witnessing yet another marriage of his parent he managed to hide behind layers of sophisticated charm.

'You're doing well,' Lily murmured, reaching down to rescue the small posy of flowers that Chloe had managed to drop twice already. 'I'm proud of you. No frowning. All you have to do is keep it up for another few hours and you're done.'

He curved his arm round her waist. 'What's my reward for not frowning?'

'Angry sex.'

There was laughter in his eyes. 'Angry sex?'

'Yes. I like that sort. It's good to see you out of control.'

'I'm never out of control.'

'You were totally out of control, Mr Zervakis, and you hate that.' She hooked her finger into the front of his shirt and saw his eyes darken. 'You are used to being in control of everything. The people around you, your work environment, your emotions—angry sex is the only time I've ever seen you lose it. It felt good knowing I was the one responsible for breaking down that iron self-control of yours. Now, stop talking and focus. This is Diandra's moment.'

The wedding went perfectly, Chloe managed to hold onto the posy and after witnessing the ceremony Lily was left in no doubt that the love between Kostas and Diandra was genuine.

'She's his favourite person,' she whispered in a choked voice and Nik turned to her, wry humour in his eyes.

'Of course she is. She cooks for him, takes care of his child and generally makes his life run smoothly.'

'That isn't what makes this special. He could pay someone to do that.'

'He *is* paying her.'

'Don't start.' She refused to let him spoil the

moment. 'Have you seen the way he looks at her? He doesn't see anyone else, Nik. The rest of us could all disappear.'

'That's the best idea I've heard in a long time. Let's do it.'

'No. I don't go to many weddings and this one is perfect.' Teasing him, she leaned closer. 'One day that is going to be you.'

He gave her a warning look. 'Lily—'

'I know, I know.' She shrugged. 'It's a wedding. Everyone dreams at weddings. Today, I want everyone to be happy.'

'Good. Let's sneak away and make each other happy.' His eyes dropped to her mouth. 'Wait here. There's one thing I have to do before we leave.' Leaving Lily standing in the shade, he walked across to his new stepmother and took her hands in his.

Lily watched, a lump in her throat, as he drew her to one side.

She couldn't hear what was said but she saw Diandra visibly relax as they talked and laughed together. And then they were joined by Kostas, who evidently didn't want to be parted from his new bride.

The whole event left Lily with a warm feeling and a genuine belief that this family really might live happily. Oh, there would be challenges of course, but a strong family weathered those together and she was sure that, no matter what had gone before, Kostas and Diandra were a strong family.

Just one dark cloud hovered on the horizon, shadowing her happiness. Now that the wedding was over, they'd both be returning to the reality of their lives.

And Nik Zervakis had no place in the reality of her life.

Still, they had one more night and she wasn't going to spoil today by worrying about tomorrow. She was lost in a private and very erotic fantasy about what the night might bring when Kostas drew her to one side.

'I have an enormous favour to ask of you.'

'Of course.' Her mind elsewhere, Lily wondered if it was time to be a bit more bold and inventive in the bedroom. Nik brought a seemingly never-ending source of energy, creativity and sexual expertise to every encounter and she wondered if it was time she took the initiative. Planning ways to give him a night he'd never forget, she remembered Kostas was talking and forced herself to concentrate.

'Would you take Chloe for us tonight? I am

thrilled she is with us, but I want this one night with Diandra. Chloe likes you. You have a way with children.'

Lily's plans for an erotic night that Nik would remember for ever evaporated.

How could she refuse when her relationship with Nik was a transitory thing and this one was for ever?

'Of course.' She hid her disappointment beneath a smile, and decided that the news that they were sharing Camomile Villa with a toddler was probably best broken when it was too late for Nik to do anything about it, so instead of enlisting his help to transport Chloe's gear across to the villa, she did it herself, sending a message via Diandra to tell him she was tired and to meet her back there when he was ready.

She'd settled a sleepy Chloe into her bed at the villa when she heard his footsteps on the terrace.

'You should have waited for me.' Nik stopped in the doorway as she put her finger to her lips.

'Shh—she's sleeping.'

'*Who* is sleeping?'

'Chloe.' She pointed to where Chloe lay, splayed like a starfish in the middle of the bed. 'It's their wedding night, Nik. They don't want to have to think about getting up to a toddler. And in case

you're thinking you don't want to get up to a toddler either, you don't have to. I'll do it.'

He removed his tie and disposed of his jacket.
'She is going to sleep in the bed?'

'Yes. I thought we could babysit her together.'
She eyed him, unsure how he'd react. 'I know this
is going to ruin our last night. Are you angry?'

'No.' He undid the buttons on his shirt and
sighed. 'It was the right thing to do. I should have
thought of it.'

'She might keep us awake all night.'

His eyes gleamed with faint mockery. 'We've
had plenty of practice.' He looked at the child on
the bed. 'Tell me what you want me to do. This
should be my responsibility, not yours. And I want
to do the right thing. It's important to me that she
feels secure and loved.'

Her insides melted. 'You don't have to "do" anything. And if you'd rather go to bed, that's fine.'

'I have a better idea. We have a drink on the
terrace. Open the doors. That way we'll hear her
if she wakes up and she won't be able to escape
without us seeing.'

'She's a child, not a wild animal.' But his deter-
mination to give his half-sister the security she
deserved touched her, and Lily stood on tiptoe
and kissed him on the cheek. 'And a drink is a

good idea. I didn't drink anything at the wedding because I was so nervous that something might go wrong.'

'I know the feeling.' He slid his hand behind her head and tilted her face to his. 'Thank you for coming with me. I have no doubt at all that the wedding was a happier experience for everyone involved because you were there.' His gaze dropped to her mouth and lingered there and her heart started to pound.

All day, she'd been aware of him. Of the leashed power concealed beneath the perfect cut of his suit, of the raw sexuality framed by spectacular good looks.

A cry from the bedroom shattered the moment and she eased away regretfully. 'Could you pick her up while I fetch her a drink? Diandra says she usually has a drink of warm milk before she goes to sleep and I'm sure today was unsettling for her.'

'It was unsettling for all of us,' he drawled and she smiled.

'Do you want warm milk, too? Because I could fix that.'

'I was thinking more of chilled champagne.' He glanced towards the bedroom and gave a resigned sigh. 'I will go to her, but don't blame me when I make it a thousand times worse.'

Perhaps because he was so blisteringly self-assured in every other aspect of his life, she found his lack of confidence strangely endearing. 'You won't make it worse.'

She walked quickly through to the kitchen and warmed milk, tension spreading across her shoulders as she heard Chloe's cries. Knowing that all that howling would simply ensure that Nik didn't offer to help a second time, she moved as quickly as she could. As she left the kitchen, the cries ceased and she paused in the doorway of the bedroom, transfixed by the sight of Nik holding his little sister against his shoulder, one strong, bronzed hand against her back as he supported her on his arm. As she watched, she saw the little girl lift her hand and rub the roughness of his jaw.

He caught that hand in his fingers, speaking to her in Greek, his voice deep and soothing.

Lily had no idea what he was saying, but whatever it was seemed to be working because Chloe's eyes drifted shut and her head thudded onto his broad shoulder as she fell asleep, her blonde curls a livid contrast to the dark shadow of his strong jaw.

Nik stood still, as if he wasn't sure what to do now, and then caught sight of Lily in the doorway. He gave her a rueful smile at his own expense and she smiled.

'Try putting her back down on the bed.'

As careful as if he'd been handling delicate Venetian glass, Nik lowered the child to the bed but instantly she whimpered and tightened her grip around his neck like a barnacle refusing to be chipped away from a rock.

He kept his hand securely on her back and cast Lily a questioning look. 'Now what?'

'Er—sit down in the chair with her in your lap and give her some milk,' Lily suggested, and he strolled onto the terrace, sat on one of the comfortable sunloungers and let the toddler snuggle against him.

'When I said I wanted to spend the evening on the terrace with a woman this wasn't exactly what I had in mind.'

'Two women.' Laughing, she sat down next to him and offered Chloe the milk. 'Here you go, sweetheart. Cow juice.'

Nik raised his eyebrows. 'Cow juice?'

'One of my friends used to call it that because whenever she said "milk" her child used to go demented.' Seeing that the child was sleepy, Lily tried to keep her hold on the cup but small fingers grabbed it, sloshing a fair proportion of the contents over Nik's trousers.

To give him his due, he didn't shift. Simply looked at her with an expression that told her she was going to pay later.

'Thanks to you I now have "cow juice" on my suit.'

'Sorry.' She was trying not to laugh because she didn't want to rouse the sleepy, milk-guzzling toddler. 'I'll have it cleaned.'

'Let me.' He covered Chloe's small fingers with his large hand, holding the cup while she drank.

Lily swallowed. 'You see? You have a natural talent.'

His gaze flickered to hers. 'Take that look off your face. This is a one-time crisis-management situation, never to be repeated.'

'Right. Because she isn't the most adorable thing you've ever seen.'

Nik glanced down at the blonde curls rioting against the crisp white of his shirt. 'I have a fair amount of experience with women and I can tell you that this one is going to be high maintenance.'

'What gave you that idea? The fact that she wouldn't stay in her bed or the fact that she spilled her drink over you?'

'For my father's sake I hope that isn't a foreshadowing of her teenage years.' Gently, he removed the empty cup from Chloe's limp fingers and handed it back to Lily. 'She's fast asleep. Now it's my turn. Champagne. Ice. You.' His gaze met hers and she saw humour and promise under layers of potent sex appeal.

Her stomach dropped and she reached and took Chloe from him. 'I'll tuck her in.'

He rose to his feet, dwarfing her. 'I'll get the champagne.'

Wondering if the intense sexual charge ever diminished when you were with a man like him, Lily tiptoed through to the bedroom and tucked Chloe carefully into the middle of the enormous bed.

This time the child didn't stir.

Lily brushed her hand lightly over those blonde curls and stared down at her for a long moment, a lump in her throat. When she grew up was she going to wonder about her mother? Did Callie intend to be in her life or had she moved on to the next thing?

Closing the doors of the bedroom, Lily took the cup back to the kitchen. By the time she returned Nik was standing on the terrace wearing casual trousers and a shirt.

'You changed.'

'It didn't feel right to be drinking champagne in wet trousers.' He handed her a glass. 'She's asleep?'

'For now. I don't think she'll wake up. She's exhausted.' She sipped the champagne. 'It was a lovely wedding. For what it's worth, I like Diandra a lot.'

'So do I.'

She lowered the glass. 'Do you believe she loves him?'

'I'm not qualified to judge emotions, but they seem happy together. And I'm impressed by how willingly she has welcomed Chloe.'

She slipped off her shoes and sat on the sun-lounger. 'I think Chloe will have a loving and stable home.'

He sat down next to her, his thigh brushing against hers. 'You didn't have that.'

She stared at the floodlit pool. 'No. I was a really sickly child. Trust me, you don't want the details, but as a result of that I moved from foster home to foster home because I was a lot of trouble to take care of. When you face the possibility of having to spend half the night in a hospital with a sick kid when you already have others at home, you take the easier option. I was never the easy option.'

He covered her hand with his. 'Was adoption never considered?'

'Older children aren't easy to place. Especially not sickly older children. Every time I arrived somewhere new I used to hope this might be permanent, but it never was. Anyway, enough of that. I've already told you far more than you ever wanted to know about me. You hate talking about family and personal things.'

'With you I do things I don't do with other people. Like attend weddings.' He turned her face to his and kissed her. 'You had a very unstable, unpredictable childhood and yet still you believe that something else is possible.'

'Because you haven't experienced something personally, doesn't mean it doesn't exist. I've never been to the moon but I know it's there.'

'So despite your disastrous relationships you still believe there is an elusive happy ending waiting for you somewhere.'

'Being happy doesn't have to be about relationships. I'm happy now. I've had a great time.' She gave a faint smile. 'Have I scared you?'

He didn't answer. Instead he lowered his head to hers again and she melted under the heat of his kiss, wishing she could freeze time and make this moment last for ever.

When she finally pulled away, she felt shaky. 'I've never met anyone like you before.'

'Cold and ruthlessly detached? Wasn't that what you said to me on that first night?'

'I was wrong.'

'You weren't wrong.'

'You reserve that side of you for the people you don't know very well and people who are trying to take advantage. I wish I were more like you. You're very analytical. There's another side of you that you don't often show to the world, but don't worry—it's our secret.'

His expression shifted from amused to guarded. 'Lily—'

'Don't panic. I still don't love you or anything. But I don't think you're quite the cold-hearted machine I did a week ago.'

I still don't love you.

She'd said the words so many times during their short relationship and they'd always been a joke. It was a code that acted as a reminder that this relationship was all about fun and sex and nothing deeper. Until now. She realised with a lurch of horror that it was no longer true.

She wasn't sure at what point her feelings had changed, but she knew they had and the irony of it was painful.

She'd conducted all her relationships with the same careful, studied approach to compatibility. David Ashurst had seemed perfect on the surface but had proved to be disturbingly imperfect on closer inspection whereas Nik, who had failed to score a single point on her checklist at first glance, had turned out to be perfect in every way when she'd got to know him better.

He'd proved himself to be both honest and unwaveringly loyal to his family.

It was that honesty that had made him hesitate before finally agreeing to take her home that night and that honesty was part of the reason she loved him.

She wanted to stay here with him for ever, breathing in the sea breeze and the scent of wild thyme, living this life of barefoot bliss.

But he didn't want that and he never would.

The following morning, Nik left Lily to pack while he returned Chloe to his father and Diandra, who were enjoying breakfast on the sunny terrace overlooking the sea.

Diandra took Chloe indoors for a change of clothes and Nik joined his father.

'I was wrong,' he said softly. 'I like Diandra. I like her a great deal.'

'And she likes you. I'm glad you came to the wedding. It's been wonderful having you here. I hope you visit again soon.' His father paused. 'We both love Lily. She's a ray of sunshine.'

Nik usually had no interest in the long-term aspirations of the women he dated, but in this case he couldn't stop thinking about what she'd told him.

I want to be someone's favourite person.

She said she didn't want a fairy tale, but in his opinion expecting a relationship to last for a lifetime was the biggest fairy tale of all. His mouth tightened as he contemplated the brutal wake-up call that awaited her. He doubted there was a man out there who was capable of fulfilling Lily's shiny dream and the thought of the severe bruising that awaited her made him want to string safety nets between the trees to cushion her fall.

'She is ridiculously idealistic.'

'You think so?' His father poured honey onto a bowl of fresh yoghurt. 'I disagree. I think she is remarkably clear-sighted about many things. She's a smart young woman.'

Nik frowned. 'She is smart, but when it comes to relationships she has poor judgement just like—' He broke off and his father glanced at him with a smile.

'Just like me. Wasn't that what you were going to say?' He poured Nik a cup of coffee and pushed it towards him. 'You think I haven't learned my lesson, but every relationship I've had has taught me something. The one thing it hasn't taught me is to give up on love. Which is good, because this twisty, turning, sometimes stony path led me to Diandra. Without those other relationships, I wouldn't be here now.' He sat back, relaxed and visibly happy while Nik stared at him.

'You're seriously trying to convince me that if you could put the clock back, you wouldn't change things? Try and undo the mistakes?'

'I wouldn't change anything. And I don't see them as mistakes. Life is full of ups and downs. All the decisions I made were right at the time and each one of them led to other things, some good, some bad.'

Nik looked at him in disbelief. 'When my mother left you were a broken man. I was scared you wouldn't recover. How can you say you don't regret it?'

'Because for a while we were happy, and even when it fell apart I had you.' His father sipped his coffee. 'I wish I'd understood at the time how badly you were scarred by it all and I certainly wish I could undo some of the damage it did to you.'

'So if you had your time again, you'd still marry her?'

'Without hesitation.'

'And Maria and Callie?'

'The same. There are no guarantees with love, that's true, but it's the one thing in life worth striving to find.'

'I don't see it that way.'

His father gave him a long look. 'When you were building your business from the ground and you hit a stumbling block, did you give up?'

'No, but—'

'When you lost a deal, did you think to yourself that there was no point in going after the next one?'

Nik sighed. 'It is *not* the same. In my business I never make decisions based on emotions.'

'And that,' his father said softly, 'is your problem, Niklaus.'

CHAPTER TEN

THE JOURNEY BACK to Crete was torture. As the boat sped across the waves, Lily looked over her shoulder at Camomile Villa, knowing she'd never see it again.

Nik was unusually quiet.

She wondered if he'd had enough of being with her.

No doubt he was ready to move on to someone else. Another woman with whom he could share a satisfying physical relationship, never dipping deeper. The thought of him with another woman made her feel ill and Lily gripped the side of the boat, a gesture that earned her a concerned frown.

'Are you sea sick?'

She was about to deny that, but realised to do so would mean providing an alternative explanation for her inertia so she gave a little nod and instantly he slowed the boat.

That demonstration of thoughtfulness simply made everything worse.

It had been so much easier to stay detached when she'd thought he was the selfish, ruthless money-making machine everyone else believed him to be.

Now she knew differently.

The drive between the little jetty and his villa should have been blissful. The sun beamed down on them and the scent of lavender and thyme filled the air, but as they grew closer to their destination she grew more and more miserable.

She was lost in her own deep pit of gloom, and it was only when he stopped at the large iron gates that sealed his villa off from the rest of the world that she realised his mistake.

She stirred. 'You forgot to drop me home.'

'I didn't forget.' He turned to look at her. 'I'll take you home if that's what you want, or you can spend the night here with me.'

Her heart started to pound. 'I thought—' She'd assumed he'd drop her home and that would be the end of it. 'I'd like to stay.'

The look in his eyes made everything inside her tighten in delicious anticipation.

He muttered something under his breath in Greek and then turned his head and focused on the driving, a task that seemed to cost him in terms of effort.

She knew he was aroused and her mood lifted and flew. He might not love her, but he wanted her. That was enough for now.

It wasn't one night.

They'd already had so much more than that.

He shifted gears and then reached across and took her hand and she looked down, at those long, strong fingers holding tightly to hers.

Her body felt hot and heavy and she stole a glance at his taut profile and knew he was as aroused as she was. In the short time they'd been together she'd learned to recognise the signs. The darkening of his eyes, the tightening of his mouth and the brief sideways glance loaded with sexual promise.

He wore a casual shirt that exposed the bronzed skin at the base of his throat and she had an almost overwhelming temptation to lean across and trace that part of him with her tongue. To tease when he wasn't in a position to retaliate.

'Don't you dare.' He spoke through his teeth. 'I'll crash the car.'

'How did you know what I was thinking?'

'Because I was thinking the same thing.'

It amazed her that they could be so in tune with each other, when they were so fundamentally different in every way.

'You need a villa with a shorter drive.'

He gave a laugh that was entirely at his own expense, and then cursed as his phone rang as he pulled up in front of the villa.

'Answer it.' She said it lightly, somehow managing to keep the swell of disappointment hidden inside.

'I'll get rid of them.' He spoke with his usual arrogant assurance before hitting a button on his phone and taking the call.

He switched between Greek and English and Lily was lost in a dream world, imagining the night that lay ahead, when she heard him talking about taking the private jet to New York.

He was flying to New York?

The phone call woke her up from her dream.

What was she doing?

Why was she hanging around like stale fish when this relationship was only ever going to be something transitory?

Was part of her really hoping that she might be the one that changed his mind?

The happiness drained out of her like air from an inflatable mattress.

She never should have come back here. She should have asked him to drop her at her flat and made her exit with dignity.

Taking advantage of the fact he was still on the phone, she grabbed her small bag and slid out of the car.

'Thanks for the lift, Nik,' she whispered. 'See you soon.'

Except she knew she wouldn't.

She wouldn't see him ever again.

He turned his head and frowned. 'Wait—'

'Carry on with your call—I'll grab a cab,' she said hastily, and then proceeded to walk as fast as she could back up his drive in the baking heat.

Why did his drive have to be so *long*?

She told herself it was for the best. It wasn't his fault that her feelings had changed, and his hadn't. Their deal had been rebound sex without emotion. She was the one who'd brought emotion into it. And she'd take those emotions home with her, as she always did, and heal them herself.

Her eyes stung. She told herself it was because the sun was bright and scrabbled in her bag for sunglasses as a car came towards her down the drive. She recognised the sleek lines of the car that had driven her and Nik to the museum opening that night. It slowed down and Vassilis rolled down the window.

He took one look at her face and the suitcase

and his mouth tightened. 'It's too hot to walk in this heat, *kyria*. Get in the car. I'll take you home.'

Too choked to argue, Lily slid into the back of the car. The air conditioning cooled her heated skin and she tried not to think about the last time she'd been in this car.

She was about to give Vassilis the address of her apartment, when her phone beeped.

It was a text from Brittany.

Fell on site, broke my stupid wrist and knocked myself out. In hospital. Can you bring clothes?

Horrified, Lily leaned forward. 'Vassilis, could you take me straight to the hospital please? It's urgent.'

Without asking questions, he turned the car and drove fast in the direction of the hospital, glancing at her in his mirror.

'Can I do anything?'

She gave him a watery smile and shook her head. At least worrying about Brittany gave her something else to think about. 'You're already doing it, thank you.'

'Where do you want me to drop you?'

'Emergency Department.'

'Does the boss know you're here?'

'No. And he doesn't need to.' She was glad she'd kept the sunglasses on. 'It was a bit of fun, Vassilis, that's all.' Impulsively she leaned forward and kissed him on the cheek. 'Thank you for the lift. You're a sweetheart.'

Scarlet, he handed her a card. 'My number. Call me when you're ready for a lift home.'

Lily located Brittany in a ward attached to the emergency department. She was sitting, pale and disconsolate, in a room where she was the only occupant. Her face was bruised and her wrist was in plaster and she had a smear of mud on her cheek.

Putting aside her own misery, Lily gave a murmur of sympathy. 'Can I hug you?'

'No, because I'm dangerous. I'm in a filthy mood. It's my right hand, Lil! The hand I dig with, type with, write with, feed myself with, punch with— Ugh. I'm so *mad* with myself. And I'm mad with Spy.'

'Why? What did he do?'

'He made me laugh! I was laughing so hard I wasn't looking where I was putting my feet. I tripped and fell down the damn hole, put my hand out to save myself and smashed my head on a pot we'd dug up earlier. It would be funny if it wasn't so tragic.'

'Why isn't Spy here with you?'

'He was. I sent him away.' Brittany slumped. 'I'm not good company and I couldn't exactly send him to pack my underwear.'

'What's going to happen? Are they keeping you in?'

'Yes, because I banged my head and they're worried my brain might be damaged.' Brittany looked so frustrated Lily almost felt like smiling.

'Your brain seems fine to me, but I'm glad they're treating you with care.'

'I want to go home!'

'To our cramped, airless apartment? Brittany, it will be horribly uncomfortable.'

'I don't mean home to the apartment. I mean home to Puffin Island. There is no point in being here now I can't dig. If I've got to sit and brood somewhere, I'd rather do it at Castaway Cottage.'

'I thought you said a friend was using the cottage.'

'Emily is there, but there's room for two. In fact it will be three, because—' She broke off and shook her head dismissively, as if realising she'd said something she shouldn't. 'Long story. My friends and I lurch from one crisis to another and it looks as if it's my turn. Can you do me a favour, Lil?'

'Anything.'

'Can you book me a flight to Boston? I'll sort out the transfer from there, but if you could get me back home, that would be great. The doctor said I can fly tomorrow if I feel well enough. My credit card is back in the apartment.' She lay back and closed her eyes, her cheeks pale against the polished oak of her hair.

'Have they given you something for the pain?'

'Yes, but it didn't do much. I don't suppose you have a bottle of tequila on your person? That would do it. Crap, I am so selfish—I haven't even asked about you.' She opened her eyes. 'You look terrible. What happened? How was the wedding?'

'It was great.' She made a huge effort to be cheerful. 'I had a wonderful time.'

Brittany's eyes narrowed. 'How wonderful?'

'Blissful. Mind-blowing.' She told herself that all the damage was internal. No one was going to guess that she was stumbling round with a haemorrhaging wound inside her.

'I want details. Lots of them.' Brittany's eyes widened as she saw the necklace at Lily's throat. 'Wow. That's—'

'It's one of Skylar's, from her *Mediterranean Sky* collection.'

'I know. I'm drooling with envy. He *bought* you that?'

'Yes.' She touched her fingers to the smooth stone, knowing she'd always remember the night he'd given it to her. 'He had one of her pots in his villa—do you remember the large blue one? She called it *Modern Minoan* I think. I recognised it and when he found out I knew Skylar, he thought I might like this.'

'So just like that he bought it for you? How the other half lives. That necklace you're wearing cost—'

'Don't tell me,' Lily said quickly, 'or I'll feel I have to give it back.' She'd intended to, but it was all she had to remind her of her time with him.

'Don't you dare give it back. You're supporting Sky. Her business is really taking off. It's thrilling for her. In my opinion she needs to ditch the guy she's dating because he can't handle her success, but apart from that she has a glittering future. That is one serious gift you're wearing, Lily. So when are you seeing him again?'

'I'm not. This was rebound sex, remember?' She said it in a light-hearted tone but Brittany's smile turned to a scowl.

'He hurt you, didn't he? I'm going to kill him.

Right after I put a deep gouge in his Ferrari, I'm going to dig out his damn heart.'

Lily gave up the exhausting pretence that everything was fine. 'It's my fault. Everything I did was my choice. It's not his fault I fell in love. I still don't understand how it happened because he is *so* wrong for me.' She sank onto the edge of the bed. 'I thought he didn't fit any of the criteria on my list, and then after a while I realised he did. That's the worst thing about it. I've realised there are no rules I can follow.'

'You're in love with him? Lily—' Brittany groaned '—a man like that doesn't *do* love.'

'Actually you're wrong. He loves his father deeply. He doesn't show it in a touchy-feely way, but the bond between them is very strong. It's romantic love he doesn't believe in. He doesn't trust the emotion.' And she understood why. He'd been deeply hurt and that hurt had bedded itself deep inside him and influenced the way he lived his life. His security had been wrenched away from him at an age when it should have been the one thing he could depend on, so he'd chosen a different sort of security—one he could control. He'd made sure he could never be hurt again.

She ached for him.

And she ached for herself.

Brittany took her hand. 'Forget him. He's a rat bastard.'

'No.' Lily sprang to his defence. 'He isn't. He's honest about what he wants. He would never mislead someone the way David did.'

'Not good enough. He should have seen what sort of person you were on that very first night and driven you home.'

'He did see, and he tried to.' Lily swallowed painfully. 'He spelled out exactly what he was offering but I didn't listen. I made my choice.'

'Do you regret it, Lil?'

'No! It was the most perfect time of my life. I can't stop wishing the ending was different, but—' She took a deep breath and pressed her hand to her heart. 'I'm going to stop doing that fairy-tale thing and be a bit more realistic about life. I'm going to "wise up" as you'd say, and try and be a bit more like Nik. Protect myself, as he does. That way when someone like David comes into my life, I'll be less likely to make a mistake.'

'What about your checklist?'

'I'm throwing it out. In the end it didn't prove very reliable.' And deep down she knew there was no chance of her making a mistake again. No chance of her falling in love again.

'Does he know how you feel?'

'I hope not. That would be truly embarrassing. Now let's forget that. You're the important one.' Summoning the last threads of her will power, Lily stood up and picked up her bag. 'I'm going to go back to our apartment, pack you a case of clothes and book you on the first flight out of here.'

'Come with me. You'd love Puffin Island. Sea, sand and sailing. It's a gorgeous place. There's nothing keeping you here, Lily. Your project is finished and you can't spend August travelling Greece on your own.'

Right now she couldn't imagine travelling anywhere.

She wanted to lie down in a dark room until she stopped hurting.

Brittany reached out and took her hand. 'Castaway Cottage is the most special place on earth. We may not have Greek weather, but right now living here is like being in a range cooker so you might be grateful for that. When I'm home, I sleep with the windows open and I can hear the birds and the crash of the sea. I wake up and look out of the window and the sea is smooth and flat as a mirror. You have to come. My grandmother thought the cottage had healing properties, remember? And it looks as if you need to heal.'

Was healing possible? 'Thanks. I'll think about it.' She gave her friend a gentle hug. 'Don't laugh at any jokes while I'm gone.'

She took a cab home and tried not to think about Nik.

Sweltering in their tiny, airless bedroom, she hunted for a top or a dress that could easily be pulled over a plaster cast.

It was ridiculous to feel this low. Right from the start, there had only been one ending.

She'd be fine as long as she kept busy.

But would he?

The next woman he dated wouldn't know about his past, because he didn't share it.

They wouldn't understand him.

They wouldn't be able to find a way through the steely layers of protection he put between himself and the world and they'd retreat, leaving him alone.

And he didn't deserve to be alone.

He deserved to be loved.

Through the window of her apartment she could see couples walking hand in hand along the street on their way to the nearest beach. Families with small children, the nice gay couple who owned Brittany's favourite bar. Everyone was in pairs. It was like living in Noah's ark, she thought gloomily, two by two.

She resisted the urge to lie down on the narrow bed and sob until her head ached. Brittany needed her. She didn't have time for self-indulgent misery, especially when this whole thing was her own fault.

She found a shirt that buttoned down the front and was folding it carefully when she heard a commotion in the street outside.

Lily felt a flicker of panic. The cab couldn't be here already, surely?

She was about to lean out of the window and ask him to wait when someone pounded on the door.

'Lily?' Nik's voice thundered through the woodwork. 'Open the door.'

The ground shifted beneath her feet and for a moment she thought there had been a minor earthquake. Then she realised it was her knees that were trembling, not the floor.

What was he doing here?

Dragging herself to the door, she opened it cautiously. 'Stop banging. These apartments aren't very well built. A cupboard fell off the wall last week.' She took in his rumpled appearance and the tension in his handsome face and felt a stab of concern. 'Is something the matter? You look terrible. Was your phone call bad news?'

'Are you ill?' He spoke in a roughened tone and she looked at him in astonishment.

'What makes you think I'm ill?'

'Vassilis told me he took you to the emergency department. You *were* very pale on the boat. You should have told me you were feeling so unwell.'

He thought she'd gone to the hospital for herself? 'Brittany is the one in hospital. She had a fall. I'm on my way there now with some stuff. I really need to finish packing. The cab will be here soon.' Knowing she couldn't keep this up for much longer, she turned away but he caught her arm in a tight grip.

'Why did you walk away from me? I thought we agreed you were going to stay another night.'

'I didn't walk. I bounded. That's what happens after rebound sex. You bound.' She kept it light and heard him curse softly under his breath.

'You didn't need to leave.'

'Yes, I did.' Aware that her neighbours were probably enjoying the show, she reached past him and closed the door. 'I shouldn't have agreed to stay in the first place. I wasn't playing by the rules. And as it happened Brittany needed me, so your phone call was perfect timing.'

'It was terrible timing.'

Discovering that being in the same room as him was even harder than not being in the same room as him, Lily walked back to the bedroom and finished packing. 'So you're flying back to New York? That sounds exciting.'

'Business demands I fly back to the US, but I have things to settle here first.'

She wondered if she was one of the things he had to settle.

He was trying to find a tactful way of reminding her their relationship hadn't been serious.

The ache inside grew worse. She tried to think of something to say that would make it easy for him. 'I have to get to the hospital. Brittany fell on site and fractured her wrist. She's waiting for me to bring her clothes and things and then I have to arrange a flight for her back to Maine because she can't stay here. She has invited me to spend August with her. I'm going to say yes.'

'Is that what you want?'

Of course it wasn't what she wanted. 'It will be fantastic.' Her control was close to snapping. 'Did you want something, Nik? Because I have to ring a cab, take some clothes to Brittany at the hospital and then battle with the stupid Wi-Fi to book a ticket and it's a nightmare. I did some research before the Internet crashed and at best it's a nine-teen-hour journey with two changes. She's going to have to fly to Athens, then to Munich where she can get a direct flight to Boston. I still have to research how she gets from Boston to Puffin Island, but I can guarantee that by the time she arrives home she'll be half dead. I'm going to fly with her because she can't do it on her own, but I hadn't exactly budgeted for a ticket to the US so I'm having to do a bit of financial juggling.'

'What if I want to change the rules?'

'Sorry?'

'You said you weren't playing by the rules.' His gaze was steady on her face. 'What if I want to change the rules?'

'The way I feel right now, I'd have to say no.'

'How do you feel?'

She was absolutely sure that was one question he didn't want answered. 'My cab is going to be here in a minute and I have to book flights—'

'I'll give you a lift to the hospital and arrange for her to use the Gulfstream. We can fly direct to Boston and she can lie down all the way if she wants to,' he said. 'And I know a commercial pilot who flies between the islands, so that problem is also solved. Now tell me how you feel.'

'Wait a minute.' Lily looked at him, dazed.

'You're offering to transport Brittany home on a private jet? You can't do that. When I told you I was going to have to do some financial juggling I wasn't fishing for a donation.'

'I know. It sounds as if Brittany's in trouble and I'm always happy to help a friend in trouble.'

It confirmed everything she already knew about him but instead of cheering her up, it made her feel worse. 'But she's my friend, not yours.'

He drew in a breath. 'I'm hoping your friends will soon be my friends. And on that topic, *please* can we focus on us for a moment?'

Her heart gave an uneven bump and she looked at him warily. 'Us?'

'If you won't talk about your feelings then I'll talk about mine. Before we left the island this morning, I had a long conversation with my father.'

Lily softened. 'I'm pleased.'

'I'd always believed his three marriages were mistakes, something he regretted, and it wasn't until today that I realised he regretted nothing. Far from seeing them as mistakes, he sees them as a normal part of life, which delivers a mix of good and bad to everyone. Yes, there was pain and hurt, but he never once faltered in his belief that love existed. I confess that came as a surprise to me.

I'd assumed if he could have put the clock back and done things differently, he would have done.'

Lily gave a murmur of sympathy. 'Perhaps it was worse for you being on the outside. You only had half the story.'

'When my mother left I saw what it did to him, how vulnerable he was, and it terrified me.' His honesty touched her but she resisted the temptation to fling her arms round him and hug him until he begged for mercy.

'You don't have to tell me this. I know you hate talking about it.'

'I want to. It's important that you understand.'

'I do understand. Your mother walked away from you. That was the one relationship you should have been able to depend on. It's not surprising you didn't believe in love. Why would you? You had no evidence that it existed.'

'Neither did you,' he breathed, 'and yet you never ceased to believe in it.'

She gave a half-smile. 'Maybe I'm stupid.'

'No. You are the brightest, funniest, sexiest woman I've met in my whole life and there is no way, *no way*,' he said in a raw tone, 'I am letting you walk out of my life.'

'Nik—'

'You asked me why I was here. I'm here because I want to renegotiate the terms of our relationship.'

She almost smiled at that. Only Nik could make it sound like a business deal. 'Is this because you know I have feelings for you and you feel sorry for me? Because, honestly, I'm going to be fine. I'll get over you, Nik. At some point I'll get out there again.' She hoped she sounded more convincing than she felt.

'I don't want you to get over me. And I don't want to think of you "out there", a pushover for anyone who decides to take advantage of you.'

'I can take care of myself. I've learned a lot from you. I'm Kevlar.'

'You are marshmallow-coated sunshine,' he drawled, 'and you need someone with a less shiny view on life to watch out for you. I don't want this to be a rebound relationship, Lily. I want more.'

Suddenly she found it difficult to breathe. 'What exactly are we talking about here? How much more?'

'All of it.' He stroked her hair back from her face with gentle hands. 'You've made me believe in something I never thought existed.'

'Fairy tales?'

'Love,' he said softly. 'You've made me believe in love.'

'Nik—'

'I love you.' He paused and drew breath. 'And unless my reading of this situation is completely wrong, I believe you love me back. Which is probably more than I deserve, but I'm selfish enough not to care about that. When it comes to you, I'll take whatever I can get.'

'Oh.' She felt a constriction in her chest. Her eyes filled and she covered her mouth with her hand. 'I'm going to cry, and you hate that. I'm really sorry. You'd better run.'

'I hate it when you cry, that's true. I don't ever want to see you cry. But I'm not running. Why would I run when the one thing in life that is special to me is right here?'

A lump wedged itself in her throat. She was so afraid of misinterpreting what he said, she was afraid to speak. 'You love me. So y-you're saying you'd like to see me again? Date?'

'No, that's not what I'm saying.' Usually so articulate, this time he stumbled over the words. 'I'm saying that you're my favourite person, Lily. And I apologise for proposing to you in a cramped airless room with no air conditioning but, as you know, I'm very goal orientated and as my goal is to persuade you to marry me then the first step is to ask you.' He reached into his pocket and pulled out a box. 'Skylar doesn't make engagement rings but I hope you'll like this.'

'You want to marry me?' Feeling as if she were running to catch up, she stared at the box. 'I'm your favourite person?'

'Yes. And when you find your favourite person it's important to hold onto them and not let them go.'

'You love me? You're sure?' She blinked as he opened the box and removed a diamond ring. 'Nik, that's *huge*.'

'I thought it would slow you down and make it harder for you to escape from me.' He slid it onto her finger and she stared at it, dazzled as the diamond caught the sun's rays.

'I'm starting to believe in fairy tales after all. I love you, too.' It was her turn to stumble. 'I knew I was in love with you, but I wasn't going to tell you. It didn't seem fair on you. You were clear about the rules right from the beginning and I broke them. That was my fault.'

With a groan, he pulled her against him. 'I knew how you felt. I was going to force you to talk to me, but then I had to take that phone call and you vanished.'

'I didn't want to make it awkward for you by

hanging around,' she muttered and he said something in Greek and eased her away from him.

'What about you?' His expression was serious. 'This isn't a first for you. You've fallen in love before.'

'That's the weird thing—' she lifted her hand to take another look at her ring, just to make sure she hadn't imagined it '—I thought I had, but then I spent time with you and told you all those things and I realised that with you it was different. I think I was in love with the idea of love. I thought I knew exactly what qualities I wanted in a person. But you can't use a checklist to fall in love. With you, I wasn't trying and it happened anyway. I need to change. I need to find a new way to protect myself.'

'I don't want you to change. I want you to stay exactly the way you are. And I can be that layer of protection that you don't seem to be able to cultivate for yourself.'

'You're volunteering to be my armour?'

'If that means spending the rest of my life plastered against you that sounds good to me.' His mouth was on hers, his hands in her hair and it occurred to her that this level of happiness was something she'd dreamed about.

'I was going to spend August on Puffin Island with Brittany.'

'Spend it with me. I have to go to New York next week, but we can fly Brittany to Maine first. I have friends in Bar Harbor. That's close to Puffin Island. While I'm at my meeting in New York you could visit Skylar. Then we can fly to San Francisco and take some time to plan our life together. I can't promise you a fairy tale, but I can promise the best version of reality I can give you.'

'You want me to go with you to San Francisco? What job would I do there?'

'Well, they have museums, but I was thinking about that.' He brushed away salty tears from her cheeks. 'How would you feel about spending more time on your ceramics?'

'I can't afford it.'

'You can now, because what's mine is yours.'

'I couldn't do that. I don't ever want our relationship to be about money.' She flushed awkwardly. 'It's important I keep custody of my rusty bike so I'm going to need you to sign one of those pre-nuptial agreement things so I'm protected in case you try and snatch everything I own.'

He was smiling. 'Pre-nuptial agreements are for people whose relationships aren't going to last and ours will last, *theé mou*.' Those words and the sincerity in his voice finally convinced her that he meant it, but even that wasn't enough to convince her this was really happening.

'But seriously, what do I bring to this relationship?'

'You bring optimism and a sunny outlook on life that no amount of money can buy. You're an inspiration, Lily. You're willing to trust, despite having been hurt. You have never known a stable family, and yet that hasn't stopped you believing that such a thing is possible for you. You live the life you believe in and I want to live that life with you.'

'So I bring a smile and you bring a private jet? I'm not sure that's an equitable deal. Not that I know much about deals. That's your area of expertise.'

'It is, and I can tell you I'm definitely the winner in this particular deal.' He kissed her again. 'The money is going to mean I can spoil you, and I intend to do that so you'd better get used to it. I thought being an artist would fit nicely round having babies. We'll split our time between the US and Greece. Several times a year we'll come back here and stay in Camomile Villa so we can see Diandra and Chloe and you can have your fill of Minoan remains.'

'Wait. You're moving too quickly for me. You have to understand I'm still getting used to the idea that I've gone from owning a bicycle, to having part ownership of a private jet.'

'And five homes.'

'I have real-estate whiplash. But at least I know how to clean them!' But it was something else he'd said that had really caught her attention. 'A moment ago—did you mention babies?'

'Have I misunderstood what you want? Am I sounding too traditional? Right now my Greek DNA is winning out,' he groaned, 'but what I'm trying to say is you can do anything you like. Make any choices you like, as long as I'm one of them.'

'You'd want babies?' She flung her arms round him. 'You haven't misunderstood. Having babies is my dream.'

His mouth was on hers. 'How do you feel about starting right away? I used to consider myself progressive, but all I can think about is how cute you're going to look when you're pregnant so I have a feeling I may have regressed to Neanderthal man. Does that bother you?'

'I've already told you I studied *homo neanderthalensis*,' Lily said happily. 'I'm an expert.'

'You have no idea how relieved I am to hear

that.' Ignoring the heat, the size of the room and the width of the bed, he pulled her into his arms and Lily discovered it was possible to kiss and cry at the same time.

'We've had fun sex, athletic sex and angry sex—what sort of sex is this? Baby sex?'

'Love sex,' he said against her mouth. 'This is love sex. And it's going to be better than anything that's gone before.'

* * * * *

MILLS & BOON®
Large Print – June 2015

THE REDEMPTION OF DARIUS STERNE
Carole Mortimer

THE SULTAN'S HAREM BRIDE
Annie West

PLAYING BY THE GREEK'S RULES
Sarah Morgan

INNOCENT IN HIS DIAMONDS
Maya Blake

TO WEAR HIS RING AGAIN
Chantelle Shaw

THE MAN TO BE RECKONED WITH
Tara Pammi

CLAIMED BY THE SHEIKH
Rachael Thomas

HER BROODING ITALIAN BOSS
Susan Meier

THE HEIRESS'S SECRET BABY
Jessica Gilmore

A PREGNANCY, A PARTY & A PROPOSAL
Teresa Carpenter

BEST FRIEND TO WIFE AND MOTHER?
Caroline Anderson

0515 Rom LP

MILLS & BOON®
Large Print – July 2015

THE TAMING OF XANDER STERNE
Carole Mortimer

IN THE BRAZILIAN'S DEBT
Susan Stephens

AT THE COUNT'S BIDDING
Caitlin Crews

THE SHEIKH'S SINFUL SEDUCTION
Dani Collins

THE REAL ROMERO
Cathy Williams

HIS DEFIANT DESERT QUEEN
Jane Porter

PRINCE NADIR'S SECRET HEIR
Michelle Conder

THE RENEGADE BILLIONAIRE
Rebecca Winters

THE PLAYBOY OF ROME
Jennifer Faye

REUNITED WITH HER ITALIAN EX
Lucy Gordon

HER KNIGHT IN THE OUTBACK
Nikki Logan

MILLS & BOON®

Why shop at millsandboon.co.uk?

Each year, thousands of romance readers find their perfect read at millsandboon.co.uk. That's because we're passionate about bringing you the very best romantic fiction. Here are some of the advantages of shopping at www.millsandboon.co.uk:

* **Get new books first**—you'll be able to buy your favourite books one month before they hit the shops

* **Get exclusive discounts**—you'll also be able to buy our specially created monthly collections, with up to 50% off the RRP

* **Find your favourite authors**—latest news, interviews and new releases for all your favourite authors and series on our website, plus ideas for what to try next

* **Join in**—once you've bought your favourite books, don't forget to register with us to rate, review and join in the discussions

Visit **www.millsandboon.co.uk**
for all this and more today!